HIT YOU WHERE YOU LIVE

LIARS AND VAMPIRES, BOOK 7

ROBERT J. CRANE

LAUREN HARPER

OSTIAGARD PRESS

HIT YOU WHERE YOU LIVE

Liars and Vampires, Book 7

Robert J. Crane w/ Lauren Harper

1

Why did I ever think it was a good idea to let the native Floridians decide what to do on an afternoon in the middle of July? I should have learned my lesson by now, six weeks into summer. I'd panted like a dog at an aquarium that was mostly outdoors, wishing some wild fish would come leaping out and splash cool, salty water over me. I'd melted at the neighborhood pool, now warm as bathwater, no refuge from the blazing heat and stifling humidity, as I lay sweating next to Xandra, avoiding touching my cell phone for fear it would burn me or worse, supply me with a heat warning telling me it would not operate until it had a chance to cool off. I'd baked during the visit to that awesome boardwalk on the Gulf of Mexico that resulted in a sunburn that seared for three days and left me feeling like a heating unit had been installed under my skin.

Floridians, man. These people are crazy.

And no one, *no one* told my northern, thick-blooded Yankee self that it was going to be just as hot at night as it was during the day in July. Sure, everyone here laughed when I told them that I was looking forward to summer. But

I thought they were joking until I got into my car one night around nine after leaving Iona's place and saw that the thermostat read ninety-eight degrees Fahrenheit.

Um...*what?*

This is what I'm dealing with. This place is insane. These people are crazy.

Oh, and the mosquitos? They exist in cloud-like formations, ever ready to devour you once the sun goes down.

So what did my crazy Floridian friends suggest for a perfectly lovely Friday afternoon in Tampa?

The beach of course. Because lessons are for people who aren't suffering from heat-stroke amnesia. By this point in the summer, I assumed we all had it.

To be honest, the beach was one of the things that I was most excited about when we moved to Florida. Dad had sold our retreat from beautiful, chilly upstate New York by promising that we would be living less than thirty minutes from some of the country's very best beaches.

And how many times had I been to visit?

Three, maybe four. Not exactly living the dream I'd envisioned when we'd fled my lying past in New York to come here. But we were making up for lost time now, even though the dream was turning into a sweaty, sticky, sand-in-places-I-didn't-want-to-think-about nightmare.

Clearwater beach was hopping. Apparently, that was normal in the summer, since it was one of the top vacation destinations. Though anyone from the north who came down here in the summer was a complete moron, in my opinion. I was pretty sure that my skin was going to slough off like melting butter when we got out of the car.

"Don't forget your sunblock," Lockwood said, leaning over the back of the seat to look at me, specifically. "And make sure to reapply it every hour. I would truly hate to see a reprisal of the last...incident."

He was wearing a brand new pair of Oakleys, cargo shorts, and a blue Hawaiian shirt with pineapples and palm trees on it. He looked like a proper tourist, though I couldn't tell if his Fae illusory abilities were masking the fact that he should have been hideously out of place here.

"Yes, Dad," I said, rolling my eyes as I waited for Laura to scooch out of the car, as I had somehow ended up stuck in the middle between her, Derrick, and Gregory.

Lockwood had enchanted the inside of the car to fit four in the back seat. He didn't have an answer, though, when Derrick had raised the point about getting pulled over by the police and how he would explain the one-too-many people in the back.

"Don't forget the things in the trunk!" he called as I crawled out into the boiling sunshine. It was so humid, this close to the water, that it was like walking through hot soup. Instantly, my back was coated in a layer of sweat, cementing my swimsuit to me. I could see the brilliantly blue water, and hear the waves lapping up against the shore. It was of little consolation, though, as a drip of warm sweat traced a path down my spine like a wet finger.

"Watch out for those guys," Xandra said, pointing at the flock of seagulls flying overhead. "They'll steal the sandwich out of your hands if you aren't paying attention."

I stared up at them. "I knew they were greedy little suckers, but seriously?"

"They would eat you alive if they could get away with it." Xandra passed a pair of brightly colored chairs to me. "Once I saw them swoop down and take a Publix Cuban sub right out of my dad's hands." She nodded as she helped Derrick pull some beach chairs out of the trunk. More than should have been able to fit. Then Gregory pulled out a large tent. I made a mental note to both scold and thank Lockwood later.

Lockwood got out of the car, taking care to avoid the oncoming traffic on the road he had parked on. "Is there anything else you need? I put sunscreen, frisbees, towels, cleaning wipes for your hands, hand sanitizer, crackers of all sorts because I didn't know who liked what, and – "

"You are the man, Lockwood!" Gregory said, hefting a bag filled with cans of Coke and Dr. Pepper into the air.

"Also," Lockwood said, "some Gatorade so you can replenish your electrolytes. I know how much you humans need those." He hesitated. "Whatever they are."

I grinned at him. "You were kind enough to fight through the crazy amounts of people on the road, bring us all the way out here, and spend ten minutes finding a spot along the sidewalk so we didn't have to walk a mile and a half to get to the beach itself. That's plenty, I think."

Lockwood smiled.

"Is there a water bottle in that cooler?" Laura asked. "I can feel my skin parching already. It really puts extra stress on your kidneys and liver, you know. I'm going to need a kale smoothie later, I think, but for now–"

"Water!" Lockwood paled. "How did I forget water?" He thrust the bundle of towels he was holding into my arms and raced around to the driver's side. "I shall return short-ly!" he called, and after Gregory closed the trunk, pulled back out into the one-lane traffic with a squeal of tires more befitting a chase scene than the omission of one specific beverage type from his packing preparations.

"I don't think I've ever seen him be such a...spaz," Xandra said, tying her periwinkle hair up into a tall messy bun on top of her head. She grinned at me as she righted herself and put her aviator sunglasses on.

"Come on, let's go find a spot," Gregory said.

Derrick hoisted the tent up onto his shoulder and fell into step beside him as the boys led us up onto the path leading over the dunes to the beach itself. Laura and Xandra grabbed the bags of towels and sunscreen, and I helped with the chairs. The sand was hot as it spilled over onto my flip flops and between my toes. Scorchingly so, like they'd been heated on the stove and poured out here on the beach.

But the breeze flowing off the water was just enough to take the edge off the heat, and the heady smell of the salty water mingled with the sunscreen from other beach goers made my heart swell with excitement. Even though I now lived in Florida, there were still days where it felt like a mini vacation.

We found a spot that wasn't entirely crowded with people a few hundred yards up the beach. A couple kids played catch with a football, shouting with delight as they passed it. Little ones built sandcastles with brightly colored plastic molds. People of all ages were spread out across the sands, lost to the world around them.

It was hard to be upset about anything when you were at the beach.

We spent a good hour, hour and a half floating in the gently lulling surf. The water was so clear I could see all the way down to the bottom, where I combed through the sand, collecting pretty shells in pink and cream and gray.

Xandra and Laura laughed, swapping beach stories about growing up in Florida. I was content to just listen and enjoy the push and pull of the waves.

I saw the bright blue of Lockwood's Hawaiian shirt appear not long after we arrived carrying a large case of water bottles. He waved at me, which I returned, then hurried away. I would have asked him to stay, but it might look weird for a middle-aged guy to be hanging out with a bunch of teenagers. Not old enough to be one of our dads, but definitely too old to be a sibling.

When Laura started to complain that her fingers were getting wrinkly, we headed back to the chairs underneath the shady area the tent provided. I sunk into mine gratefully, my muscles pleasantly sore and stretched. I knew that I was going to sleep well tonight. Laura tossed me a cold water bottle, already slick with condensation.

"The guys drank half the drinks already," Xandra said, pawing through the cooler. "Gregory! I'm going to kill you if you drank all the Dr. Pepper!"

Gregory turned to look, and the ball that Derrick had just tossed smacked him right upside the head.

Derrick dissolved into a fit of laughter, and Gregory started yelling at both Xandra and Derrick.

With their grousing as my beach soundtrack, I settled in the chair, lowering the back so that I was almost horizontal. The wind rustled my loose auburn curls, brushing them over my sunburnt cheeks that I had forgotten to slather in sunscreen like Lockwood told me to.

"You know, it's too bad your boyfriend couldn't come," Xandra said to me, her Dr. Pepper fizzing as she popped open the can. "I can't imagine not being able to enjoy days like this."

"I think he'd like to be here," I said. "But not bad enough to brave spontaneous combustion."

Xandra snickered.

I stretched my arms up over my head and smiled. "Plus, he is super cranky during the day."

We all shrieked as a ball landed nearby, bouncing in the

sand, spraying us all with sand and bits of shells. Xandra promptly picked it up and tossed it back out of the tent at Gregory. "Watch it!"

"Sorry!" Gregory hollered, trying to suppress his laughter. Derrick was wiping tears from his eyes, doubled over in laughter.

I settled back down and laid my head back against the chair, sighing with contentment. I wasn't sure when the last time I felt this relaxed. Xandra turned on some music, a J-Pop group, and cracked open a manga, humming along with the song. Laura unrolled her towel and draped it on the ground just outside the shade, tanning underneath the blasting sunshine.

It wasn't the first time that I wished that Mill was just a normal guy and not a vampire. It robbed us of something that normal couples got to experience. Like going to an amusement park together. Disney World was out of the question, regardless of the fact it was less than two hours away. And no romantic walks on the beach...

Unless...

Would he ever be interested in a *moonlit* stroll along the shore? No fear of the sun, but the same gentle breeze, the sweet smell of the water, the feel of the sand between our toes?

My cheeks flushed as I thought about holding his hand as we walked, talking about life in general. Having a few quiet moments to ourselves.

I heard Derrick and Gregory wander back over to the tent, laughing and carrying on. They opened the cooler, grabbed some snacks, and sunk down into their own chairs.

"So did you guys see that episode of–"

"Don't say anything!" Gregory cried. "I haven't seen it yet! No spoilers!"

Derrick laughed. "Sorry, man. I assumed you of all people would have seen it."

"I was at work, dude!" Gregory said. "You know, like a responsible adult?"

"Does working at a used video game store count as real work?" Xandra asked. I heard her turn a page in her manga.

"Hey, now," Gregory said. "I make pretty good money. And I happen to be very knowledgeable about the product we sell."

"Because you don't have a life, yes," Xandra teased.

I opened one eye to see Gregory's face turn scarlet as he rounded on her with a pointed finger. "Says the otaku with the manga!"

Derrick was standing off to the side, staring back and forth between them as if he were watching a tennis match, sipping his Coke with mild amusement.

Xandra shrugged. "I'm comfortable with my inherent geekiness."

Gregory glared at her through squinted eyes. "At least I have a job."

"I do, too," she said. "At my mom's noodle place."

"That doesn't count."

"Does so! I make money! Isn't that the definition of a job?"

"Yeah, but I got my job all on my own! I didn't need my mom to–"

"Hey, look at those guys that are like, completely covered up," Laura said, sitting up on her elbows, pointing up the beach. "Is that motorcycle gear?"

"Kinda hot to be wearing all black like that..." Xandra said. She pulled down her sunglasses, squinting against the bright sunshine.

Gregory's annoyance seemed to sizzle out as he stared out over the sandy shore. "Weird."

No, I realized, not just weird. My stomach dropped like I missed a step as I followed their gaze.

Unworldly. As in...not of the human world.

No. It couldn't be.

Vampires.

2

That was when the screaming began.

"Vampires!" I cried, stumbling as I tried to scramble out of my chair.

"What?" Xandra was on her feet in a second.

"Wait, those guys?" Gregory asked.

They were wearing motorcycle helmets, their visors reflective and hiding their faces. Their biker gear was skin tight, like spandex but durable for road wear. And it was all jet black. They were moving across the beach way faster than any normal person would be able to cut through sand, headed right toward us. Other beach goers shrieked and dove out of their way. The peaceful scene had turned completely chaotic in less than a second.

"Run!" I said, taking off down the beach toward the next beach access point, the others falling in behind me.

Didn't matter. They caught up to us so fast I heard Xandra cry out in pain before I had run ten feet. Wheeling around, I saw one of the vamps already dragging her back up the beach toward the street.

"No!" I shouted, launching myself at the vampire.

It went about as well as I'd come to expect from the times I'd tried to take on a vampire unarmed. He barely turned to look at me, shoving me away as I got close, and continued on, unimpressed. I stumbled backward, landing on my ass in the sand.

Another one of the vampires ran right past me to where Derrick was churning up sand, cutting through the dunes. It tackled him to the ground and they both went down in a spray of grains. Derrick cried out in anger, his muscles flexing and straining as he attempted to shove the vampire off. No effect. If anything, it only agitated the vamp, who tried to drag Derrick to his feet. Derrick, not willing to just go along, pulled back his free arm, and punched the vampire right in the neck. The slap of knuckles against leather snapped across the sands.

Though I couldn't see his face beneath the motorcycle helmet, the vampire hesitated, stunned, at least for a second. Long enough for Derrick to exclaim something victorious, but not long enough for the vampire to not retaliate by punching him in the gut, doubling him over.

A shriek drew my attention, and I wheeled around to see another vampire dragging Laura toward the path by her hair. She was kicking and screaming, yanking at the vampire's hand knotted in her blonde braids. She was putting up enough of a fight to slow him down, but not nearly enough to stop him.

I gritted my teeth and jumped on the back of the vampire dragging Laura. I had no plan but to make myself the fly in their ointment, the cloud of mosquitos at their barbecue. Absent a stake, a weapon, I was little more than a pain in their proverbial rectum, and I knew it.

Still, I couldn't just let them drag my friends away without putting up a fight.

The vampire grabbed the strap of my swimsuit, yanked me off, and tossed me into the sand easily. I planted in the dunes, rolling out of it shoulder-first and coming back to my feet using a maneuver Mill had taught me. I paused, considering what I'd just seen.

The vamp had thrown me without much effort. He could have spiked me face-first in the sand, breaking my neck. Instead he'd tossed me like a pizza, without much malice, a strange choice. Or just snagged me over his shoulder and dragged me along with the rest of them.

Why weren't the vamps fighting back? And why were they so determined to take my friends?

My stomach plummeted.

My friends. That was the point, wasn't it?

"Cassie!"

I wheeled around, my heart soaring.

Lockwood had returned, a cooler in his hands. His eyes fell on the masked vampires, his face hardened, and he took off after the one carrying Gregory. The vampires swiftly took notice of Lockwood, and by their reaction, they knew who he was. They started to hurry their steps, blurring through the sand, sending it flying everywhere in their hurried retreat.

The vampire who had Laura halted after seeing Lockwood, hesitating for a second.

It was all I needed.

I reached my hand up behind the vampire's head, getting enough of a handhold to shove with all my might. I threw the helmet forward. I saw skin and hair for a brief second as the helmet slid off, but as soon as the sun saw it, the vampire burst into flames.

I grabbed Laura, the vampire's fingers still knotted in her hair. After a few tense seconds, struggling to extract her from the vamp, burning from the head like a candle, I won the fight. The vampire turned and bolted, flaming, toward the surf.

"You got him," Laura breathed, face blotchy and red. She looked at me with wide, terrified eyes. "And me."

"Stay here," I said. "I don't think I'll have another opening like that again."

The other vampires paused, attention drawn by the shriek of their friend. Lockwood managed to skid through a mound of sand and close the distance between himself and the nearest of the leather-clad vamps. From out of nowhere, or rather, from out of his complete lack of sleeves on the Hawaiian shirt, he produced a stake and shoved it into the back of the vampire carrying Gregory.

The vamp crumpled to the ground, and Gregory shrieked as black blood started to ooze from the wound. He fell off the vampire's shoulder and puffed into the sand as the body began to collapse in on itself. Luckily, the beach was just about clear by now, sparing us from hearing any stories on the five o'clock news about how a man had turned into a blob of black mucus. Still, the cops were bound to find it, and there was no explanation for that sort of thing. Lockwood must have realized this, because he bent over the body, touched it with the tip of his finger, and it vanished under a fae illusion.

"Lockwood!" I called. "Xandra!"

Two vamps remained; one had Derrick, the other was carrying Xandra toward the crossover back to the asphalt parking area. Xandra was struggling against her captor, but it was futile, like a baby wrestling against a professional bodybuilder. Her pale hand kept landing against his leather-clad back, again and again, to no effect. Lockwood was after them, but the likelihood he'd be able to take on both now that they knew he was coming? Almost zero, I judged.

"They're going to get away," Laura mumbled into her hands.

I looked around frantically for something, anything that could help me. Aluminum-framed chairs, empty water bottles, Bluetooth speakers...nothing that would actually help against creatures of the night. I took a deep breath and started toward the vampires when my foot caught on something sharp. "Ow!" I stumbled, and turned around to see what I had stepped on.

A broken shell. Sharp.

I stooped, grabbed it, and tore off after the vampire fighting with Derrick.

The vampire had won that struggle. Derrick was nearly unconscious, sagging on the vamp's shoulder, with a really nasty cut under his eye and a red slash from his collarbone to his opposite shoulder. The vamp's back was to me, and honestly, he really didn't seem to care what I was doing, so he didn't even react when I huffed my way up and leapt at him, dragging the pointed end of the broken shell across the back of the biker suit. The fabric resisted in some places, but a hole near the spine appeared, and the vampire whipped around.

"Why you little–"

But the sun saw the skin, too, and the vampire yowled as a gout of flame burst from the hole. I watched as he dropped Derrick and made a dash for the ocean, throwing himself into the water. It sizzled and bubbled around him, churning as he thrashed frantically in the shallow waves.

The water did nothing to put out the flames. The suit seemed to belch flames from the joints, the wrists, the feet, and within a few seconds, it collapsed like the vampire within just dissolved into nothingness. Which he sort of had. It washed limply onto the sands with the next wave.

I sprinted for the crossover, flip-flops slapping against the sands, sending grains flying everywhere. I made it with a faster time than I'd ever logged in any gym class, ever, and found myself looking at the horrifying spectacle.

In the parking lot, Lockwood was fighting two leather-shielded vamps beside a van. Must have been the backup, because they hadn't been on the beach with the rest. The van's side door was wide open, and empty, ready for the vampire that carried Xandra over his shoulder. Her pale, milky skin contrasted against the black leather, and she was twisting and writhing against his impossibly strong grip. She was putting up a good fight, but it was doing nothing but stalling him, tossing him off balance by throwing all her weight in one direction, then another. He almost toppled over, righting himself just before reaching the point of no return. He tried to club her, and it seemed to stun Xandra, her eyes blinking against the strong, cuffing blow.

I caught up just shy of the van, and tried to land a hit on the arm wrapped around Xandra. It was like hitting steel; my hand bounced off, throbbing with pain. Lockwood was tied up dealing with the backup, who were keeping out of his reach. None of my other friends had made it off the beach yet.

"Cassie!" Xandra moaned, reaching out toward me with her free arm. Blood trickled down her forehead. She seemed dazed, probably concussed.

This attack happened in broad daylight. They didn't care who would see it. Whoever was behind this was bold.

I hit the vampire in the small of his back and he barely staggered. Once more, it was like striking a wall. My knuckles hurt, blood welled from little scrapes where I'd hit impossibly hard vampire skin.

This was a losing fight. I needed to be faster, stronger, better. To have weapons at hand that could damage vampires. The sort of things I would have had on hand weeks ago, when I'd taken on the vampire Lord of Tampa. Before I thought I'd won, and gotten sloppy and complacent. Before I started going to the beach without a stake at hand.

Now my friends were going to pay for my sloppiness. Xandra barely struggled against the vampire, her head bobbing as he carried her the last feet to the van. Acid burned in my stomach, and in spite of the fatigue settling over me from the run, and the fighting, and the feeling of desperation knowing that I was outmatched...

...A new resolve crept into me, too.

I had to save her.

3

I still had the shell knife in my hand, clenched tightly in my fist. Blood trickled out of my palm where it had dug into my skin as I ran. I had forgotten all about it, but now fatigue was setting in, and along with it, pain that had been held at bay by the hard dump of adrenaline that came with the fear in a life-threatening situation.

Xandra's purple-blue hair was all a mess, in her face as she struggled weakly against the vampire who was dragging her the last steps to the waiting van. As he tried to throw her in, she caught herself on the door, refusing to go gently into that good (creature of the) night's van.

"Hang on, Xandra!" I launched myself at the vampire, slashing with the shell. The vampire stepped easily out of the way, not letting go of her.

But Xandra was still gripping onto the side of the van, and she shrieked in pain as her arm unwillingly parted with the side of the van.

My stomach clenched with nausea as I heard a snap. Xandra made a mewling noise, a sort of gasping cry. I gritted my teeth and tried the shell again on the arm of the vampire, but the vampire was too quick. He dodged my attack, sliding to the side, Xandra still on his shoulder.

"You can't protect her," the vamp said, voice muffled by the helmet and visor. I couldn't even see his face beneath it all, but he had an accent. "No human could."

"Lucky I'm not a human, then." Lockwood appeared behind him, a nasty gash across his cheek, silver blood dripping down onto his Hawaiian shirt. He grabbed the vampire before it could spin, taking it off balance.

As soon as its back was turned, cinched tightly in Lockwood's grip, I ran in and wrenched the motorcycle helmet off. Flames belched forth starting at the neck, and Xandra rolled off, landing with a scream on her wounded arm as the vampire lit off like a sparkler.

Lockwood tossed him aside as he burst into flames. The vamp's screams of agony gave way to the shriek of sirens under the stifling sun. "I have to go," Lockwood said, gasping for air, his silver blood turning the Hawaiian shirt a terrible, glistening shade. "They won't find bodies. Tell the police that they took off."

I was panting, kneeling down beside Xandra, who was moaning. "Are you going to be okay?"

"I am not badly injured," Lockwood said, "but dealing with the police would put more strain on my illusions than I think advisable." He looked truly torn, as though he wanted to stay and run, all at once.

Gregory reached us, and paled when he saw Xandra. Then more when he saw Lockwood and his silver blood. "Are they okay?"

"I think Xandra broke her arm," I said, the sick feeling in my stomach coming back. "When the vampire tried to dodge my attack." I looked up at Lockwood; he was truly torn. "Don't worry, we'll be fine," I said. "Go."

And he did, vanishing on the spot.

It was good that he did, because a moment later police cars turned onto the street, coming to a screeching stop behind the van. Their sirens rang loud, and their blue and red lights flashed brightly, though they were dimmed by the sun's blazing light, as we waited, Xandra's choked sobs of pain barely muffled by the howling klaxons.

4

We got the rundown of usual questions from the police. My friends were good little secret keepers, only giving the police the information that we knew for sure. Still, we were stuck answering questions under the blazing sun in our swimwear. My skin had turned lobster-like, a crisis blanket my only shield from turning my four-alarm blazing burn into a ten-alarm one. I was tempted to ask the fire department, who had also showed up, to hose me off while the cops finished interrogating me.

"How did you guys get to the beach today??" the officer, a tall and thin fellow, asked me.

"A friend dropped us off," I said. All truth, no lies.

"Do you know who these people are that attacked you?"

"I have never met any of those people in my life." The truth, but not the whole truth. I felt a little sick with myself for how quickly I fell back into that trap, and how easily I could still do it without batting an eye. But what was the alternative? *Yeah, we got whacked by vampires, and my faerie friend flew off because you guys were coming. Could you drop me off back home? No? You're taking me to the asylum? Makes sense.*

Laura exhaled heavily beside me, casting off her crisis blanket once the cops had finished with us. We were sitting in a circle, the four of us that remained, on our chairs, which one of the cops had kindly retrieved from the beach so we didn't have to sit on the blazing asphalt. "So Xandra's going to be okay?"

"I guess," I said, wiping away some of the condensation on the side of my water bottle. "The EMT said they had to get her to the hospital so they could set her arm."

"I did that once when I was eleven," Derrick said. "Fell out of a tree. Lemme tell you. That hurts."

"It definitely looked broken," Gregory agreed. "Like...I am gonna have nightmares about that."

I understood. I had been trying to push the images out of my head for the last hour. We all fell silent. None of us really wanted to address the real reason why we were still stuck waiting for police to ask us any other questions before we were allowed to leave.

But Derrick, the kid who continued to surprise me with his bravery, furrowed his brow and said, "This...this was a legit attack."

"A vamp attack," Gregory said, "in the middle of the day? That's a pretty ballsy move, bro."

Laura frowned as she looked at me. "Ugh, vampires. I thought you wiped out Lord Draven."

"I did," I said. "I stood there and watched the sun burn them all."

"Okay, so the old vamps with a grudge are dead. So who'd you piss off this time?" Gregory asked.

I shot him a nasty look. "Why do you assume that I did anything wrong?"

He shrugged. "Just checking."

"There were no vampires left, okay?" I said. "Not organized, anyway. Iona and Mill said so. Tampa is a certified vamp-free town." I squirmed, because obviously the evidence of my eyes said differently. "Or it was."

"Yeah, they looked pretty organized to me," Laura said, frowning. I saw her reach up and gingerly touch the back of her head. I was surprised that she hadn't lost half of her hair when the vampire was dragging her.

"They were definitely organized," I said. My stomach twisted in knots. "They came in the middle of the day, they came ready for daylight. They knew what they were dealing with, aside from Lockwood...if he hadn't come back with the water just then, we all would have been screwed."

Derrick's eyes narrowed as he stared at the sandy ground.

"Not you," he said, looking up at me. "They left you alone, didn't they?"

I looked away. So that wasn't all in my head. A lump formed in my throat, and I was suddenly queasy. They went after my friends. These people, who have nothing in common with one another...

Nothing in common apart from being friends with me.

That realization hit like a punch to my gut.

I hadn't wiped out all of the vampires that day in Tampa. In fact, one had definitely survived that had a very strong grievance with me.

Jacquelyn.

5

Later that night, after being released by the police to my frantic parents, I drove through Tampa following the river road that led to Iona's little yellow house. It had been a scorching day of sun, sunburn, and oh, parental concern once the police released me. Fortunately, my parents were now in on the supernatural secrets that wove themselves into every facet of my Florida life, and after a little begging Mom had let me borrow Dad's car for this sojourn. As I pulled into the driveway, all the lights were on, the doors and windows open, and Iona's little Volkswagen Beetle was parked in the driveway. The crickets chirped as I shut my door, the light spilling out of the house my guide up the front walk.

Iona appeared in shadow like a specter, her long, silvery blonde hair shining in the backlight. It was a loose braid that swung over her shoulder as she leaned outside, peering at me. "Cassie?"

"Sorry for showing up unannounced," I said, walking through the front door.

"I was hoping you'd show up," she said. "We left off on

episode seven of *The Great British Bake Off*, after all, and I kinda want to see what happens next. Or! We could go to that café where they make those scones you like? Oh! Or we could play that card game again! What was it called? Flux?"

"Ahhh..." I was caught a little off guard by this; I had been hanging out with Iona lately, and under normal circumstances, I would have been perfectly happy to do...well, any of these things. Unfortunately... "I actually have an ulterior motive for coming over tonight, Iona..." And I explained what had happened at the beach.

"And they only attacked your friends?" Iona was left staring at me through thinly slitted eyelids, deep in concentration as she considered what I'd just told her.

"'Attacked' is a strong word for it," I said. "'Kidnapped' is closer to the mark. Tried to, anyway, and left me almost alone."

Iona slowly made her way to the window, looking out into the darkness. Insect noises hummed from outside, and she slammed the sill. "Sorry. Like I said, didn't know you were coming and mosquitos just ignore me."

"Yeah, I suppose you're birds of a feather that way," I said. "Same beverage preferences and all that."

Iona nodded absently. "I don't get it. Why would vampires kidnap your friends? We killed Lord Draven. That's the end of his power in Tampa, and there's no one left to hold a grudge about it."

I felt a squeezing pain inside. "Uhmm...do you remember Jacquelyn?"

"Tall? Black hair? Practically born to be a vampire, and then achieved her destiny?" Iona said. "Yeah. I thought she was killed at Draven's."

I hung my head. "I saw her get away in the elevator."

Iona groaned, and I was quickly reminded of her prickly side. "Cassie, you let her get away?"

"I know, I know," I said. "Spare me the lecture, will you? I realize it was stupid. But here's my question – how could a nobody vamp from New York organize something like this?"

"How did she get in like Flynn with Lord Draven?" Iona sank down on her brightly colored, summery couch. The pillows had palm trees embroidered on them. I kid you not. "Are you sure it's her?"

I shook my head. "No. It's possible it could be someone else. I just don't know who."

"Exactly. Why would the new guy have any beef with you...?" Iona asked, more to herself than to me.

"New guy?" I asked.

Iona nodded, staring at a blank spot on the wall. "Yeah. There's only so much land. If a vampire territory is vacant, another Lord will step in to fill it. Which is what's happened here. Why?" She cocked her head at me. "What did you think would happen?"

I groaned. "I thought Tampa was, like...a free city now or something."

Iona snorted. "When was the last time you heard of a cattle baron dying and people just turning loose his livestock and turning his ranch into national forest?"

My face crystallized into a mask of disgust. "That's so insulting. We're not cattle."

Her eyes narrowed. "You are to vampires."

"Who is this 'new guy?'" I asked, feeling a little sick. I went through that whole battle with Draven, thinking maybe my life would go vampire-free with the exception of Iona and Mill, and here I was facing another vampire Lord. Honestly, I saw now why America had told the monarchy to kiss off in 1776. Though we were worse than serfs to these vamps; we were food.

"No idea," Iona said. "I try to stay out of all that nonsense. But if I had to guess, I'd probably say that they would come from Jacksonville. Or Orlando. Maybe Savannah, Tallahassee...Miami..."

My stomach dropped. "The Lord of the Miami territory could take over Tampa?"

She shrugged. "It could happen, yeah."

"But we don't know for sure."

Iona nodded. "You know who might know?"

"Please don't say Mill." I closed my eyes. "I'm trying to avoid...y'know. Worrying him." I would probably have to tell him eventually, but I was also dreading it.

"Good luck with that," Iona muttered under her breath. She shifted on the couch, her face a mask of concentration. "You know who might have the answer?"

"Who?"

"The one person who has all the info we could ever want." Her eyes lit up, and I could tell she was pleased, probably at the thought of me coming to her for vampire help over Mill. The amber in her eyes shone in the reflected light. "We should talk to the Oracle."

She was not in a wheelchair, and I was not Batman.

Back to Ikea we went. It was twenty minutes until they closed when we strolled through the front doors. The death looks we got from the workers told us that they had already started to close up and mentally check out for the night, and us being there was preventing them from getting home ten minutes earlier than usual. Such was the life of a purveyor of cheap Swedish furniture. And retail workers everywhere, really.

"We're going to have to make this quick," I whispered to Iona as we hopped on the escalator to the showroom. It whirred quietly under the hum of fluorescent lights, the store about as dead as ever I'd seen it.

"Or what?" Iona brushed her platinum hair back. "I'd like to see them make me leave before I'm done deciding between the Ektorp sofa or the Klippan."

My eye twitched slightly. Who knew the names of these products? Iona, apparently. We hurried back toward the kitchen area, noting that there were very few people in the aisles. It made it easy for us to duck inside the pantry that we had visited the time before, for Iona to mutter something again, and for the same portal to appear as the first time we went through.

Portal jumping was just...not my thing. But I still stepped through first, Iona following closely. Once through, I blinked and stared around. Last time, we had ended up in a grand valley with beautiful sun casting shadows everywhere, waterfalls pouring down on either side of us. A floating castle had waited.

This time there were no grand valleys with waterfalls, nor was there a floating castle anywhere in sight.

Nope. We were just in a tiny, but well decorated, studio apartment in what looked like...

"Is that Tokyo Tower?" I asked, pointing at the red and white nestled amongst more buildings than I could count. An enormous picture window provided a very different sort of view for this visit.

"Yep," came a voice from behind me.

I whipped around and saw the Oracle sitting – no, hovering – above an expensive gaming chair, in black and bright blue, in front of the mother of all PCs. Three monitors sprawled across the desk, with a keyboard with glowing green keys beneath. A black mouse with bright red light zoomed across the longest mouse pad that I had ever seen, and the Oracle's other hand was hovering over the W, A, and D keys.

"What do you need?" she asked, glancing over her shoulder at us. Her eyes caught me off guard again. The irises were soft purple, but her pupils were the most striking navy blue that I had ever seen. Not to mention that her lashes were still violently pink. She was wearing an oversized hoodless pullover sweatshirt in pale grey, black skintight leggings, and was barefoot.

"Nice hair," Iona commented, strolling over to the desk. She was taking this rather well, despite the fact that this place was entirely different from how it was last time we had seen her. Was that a thing that happened in this place? It shifted from some otherworldly spectacle to a prosaic-ish Tokyo apartment on command?

The Oracle grinned. Her hair, which was previously cotton candy blue with pink streaks throughout was now a deep, dark green, and hung in loose curls over her shoulders. "Yeah? It's one of my favorites. Just changed it before I hopped on." She wore a pair of the most expensive earbud headphones, one of which was stuck in her ear, and had a microphone nice enough for a live streamer. "Yeah, hold on," she said toward her computer. "I'm AFK."

"What?" Iona asked.

The Oracle rolled her eyes, chomping down on something in her mouth.

I blinked. She was chewing gum. One of the most powerful magical beings that I had ever met...was chewing gum.

"I'm just about ready to go on a raid with my guild," the Oracle said as if it were the most obvious thing in the world. "So if you could hurry up and tell me – Listen, I heard you. Just hold your mounts." She turned back to us, tossing her green curls over her shoulder. "Could you hurry up and ask me about your human problems already?"

I shook my head a little. "I...don't even know what to say."

The Oracle turned in her chair to look at us. She crossed one leg over the other, chomping her gum, arching a brow at me. "What? Is this throwing you off? You didn't expect me to have hobbies?"

"No, not really," I said. "Sort of thought you just sat

around, reading ancient tomes, and hanging out with other magical creatures. Maybe...ran a unicorn petting zoo in your free time, I dunno." I stared at the tri-screen. "What even is that?"

She smirked at me, her eyes narrowing mischievously. "This year? It's WoW. Last year? Destiny 2. Before that? I was really into organic tomato growing. Can't stay predictable. I've lived for so long that I've tried all the classic stuff, y'know? Went through a skateboarding phase in the eighties. That was dope. And a farming phase for, like...millennia, really. Have you seen the lemon tree out on my balcony? Had it for almost a hundred years."

I opened my mouth to speak when she spun her chair back toward her computer.

"Yes, I know, Kronk. I just finished the buffs. Chill." She hesitated, then breathed, "What a choadbag." Then, with a look at me, she said, "I'm waiting for you to ask about the new vamps in town."

It took me off guard, again, that she knew exactly why we were there. I shouldn't have been surprised. She knew pretty much everything the last time I saw her. Iona crossed her arms over herself and looked pointedly at me.

"Oh, and let me congratulate you on taking out Draven," the Oracle said, grinning. "I was never all that fond of him. He didn't like my counsel, even though I was right every time...about everything." She chuckled, then turned back to her keyboard, tapping away.

It was both awkward and annoying standing there, waiting and wondering if I had her attention. "Is Jacquelyn involved?" I asked, figuring it was better to just be outright with her. Beating around the bush was a waste of time for her and for us.

"Don't you know?" the Oracle asked, not even looking at

me. She just kept tapping away. I wasn't even sure she was talking to me until she turned her blue pupils onto mine.

"Do you have a potion of prolonged power?" Iona was staring intensely at the screen, then leaned over to stare at the Oracle's cleric avatar. She had her inventory screen open and was scrolling through.

"Good point," the Oracle said. "Knew I was forgetting something in all this hubbub. Yes, Kronk, thank you, I'm a noob, whatever."

I gaped at Iona. "Wait, what? How do you know – "

Iona looked at me, looked away, and shrugged. "How do you think we met?"

"I..." I started.

The Oracle winked at me. "We are creatures of the night, little Seelie. What do you think we do? Party?" She lifted a mug that definitely had not been anywhere in sight, and sipped from it.

There was that nickname again.

Iona nodded. "My guild raids on Tuesdays and Thursdays."

"I can't even..." I said, turning away from the pair of them. They were not taking any of this seriously.

"Oh, quit your pouting," the Oracle said. "Constant of the universe: Teenagers. So whiny."

"I'm not whining," I said.

The Oracle arched a brow.

"You are pouting, though." She tilted her head to the side. "And I can understand why. You're upset about your old friend."

"So she is involved...?" I asked.

"All good things come to an end," the Oracle said. "Like the bellbottoms trend. And the no-fat diet fad. And the fact that the Tampa vampire territory is unclaimed."

"What does that have to do with–?"

"Pretty much everything," the Oracle said, sipping from her mug again. She set it down and put her hand back on her mouse. "Nature abhors a vacuum, and living creatures abhor a power vacuum. Iona was right. The new boss, not quite the same as the old boss? It's Lord Varycas."

I turned to Iona. "Miami," she said, reading the question on my face.

"Great," I said. I thought the name sounded familiar. I'd spent a night in Miami not that long ago, and chaos had, of course, ensued.

"And Varycas has met your little friend," the Oracle said, her smile tightening. "Would you care to guess what they might have talked about?"

No mysteries there, but my stomach buzzed with worry nonetheless. "Uhmm...the finer points of parliamentary procedure for their vampire club meetings?"

Oracle didn't laugh; she barely even smirked. Instead, she went back to her game, which told me everything I needed to know.

Jacqueline was working with the new vampire lord in Tampa, one who already probably had a grudge against me for what I'd done when I'd visited his territory. Suddenly the mystery of what had happened on the beach that afternoon was no longer a mystery at all.

Now the only mystery left was...what would they do next?

7

"So I have a question..." I asked, once we were safely back at Iona's sweltering home, "if Varycas and Jacquelyn are in cahoots already, then do I need to try and make myself known before she twists his image of me, and we have a whole Draven situation all over again?"

Iona sighed, shaking her head. "Do you really want to get involved in vampire politics again?"

"I have been already, against my will...again," I said. "If Jacquelyn is the one behind the attack."

Iona nodded slowly. "She really hates you, doesn't she?"

"No kidding." I sagged back against the couch.

"I just can't believe you would want to meet with this Lord when you murdered the last one," she said. "Or that he'd want to meet with you. As plans go, this is not among your best."

"I'm just trying to figure out how to drag myself out of this mess before it devolves into another crisis like last time," I said. The cicadas were screeching outside, something that I learned meant that it was really hot. No duh. I fluttered the front of my tank top, wiping my forehead with the back of my other hand. "You really don't believe in air conditioning, huh?"

"You are the only human who has spent time here," she said, "and heat doesn't bother me."

"You're the reverse Elsa, I see," I said, still fanning myself. "I do note that heat must bother you at least a little, given how vamps burn up under the sun."

"Light does not equal heat."

"Pretty sure it does," I said softly, "but I guess I'm not the best student of science."

"Speaking of science," Iona said, "you know that this other Lord is way open about his eating of humans, right?"

"I remember," I said regretfully. "Not sure what that has to do with science, though."

"Cause and effect," Iona said. "You got into a squabble in his territory. He is a vampire supremacist. Ergo, you schedule a meet with him, and you get invited for dinner." She whirled her hand in a slow circle, like a spinning wheel. "Literally."

"Ugh. And the 'squabble?' That was totally not me. That was Mill," I said. And maybe me, a little. Damn. A tiny...ish lie. From a certain perspective.

"I don't think it being your boyfriend's fault is going to make things any easier. Also, I'm not a fan of his," Iona said, "but you might want to tell him. Now that you know for sure."

I sighed. She had a point. "It's been so nice these last few months. I thought we were free from all of this."

Iona nodded. "I know. I had hoped so, too. I'm sorry."

"It's not your fault," I said.

"That said," Iona went on, "back to your original question – there is a prescribed method for truce meetings, yes."

My ears perked up. "Wait, you're serious?"

She gave me a hard look. "I don't want to go through with Varycas what we did with Draven, so...yes. I am serious. It may be worth a try. Provided it's not a dinner meeting."

"Yeah, I'm not looking to be dinner," I said. "Or have dinner, which I assume is B-positive consomme. So...truce. How? What do we do?"

"It's complicated," Iona said, "but it starts with Varycas's current, established position as Lord of Miami. When there's a territory vacated, it doesn't stay unoccupied for long. They are taken and held by conquest. Since Draven fell, it was only a matter of time before someone stepped up to take the mantle."

"Okay, so why did Varycas get it?"

"There is...a highly ritualized style for how everything unfolds. For both war and peace."

"Okay," I said. "I conquered the last vampire Lord, so does that mean that I can engage in this process? Hopefully come to a peaceful solution?"

"No, you're cattle," she replied flatly.

"Oh, thanks," I said.

"Well, not to me," she said. "But to Varycas."

"I killed his rival," I said, choosing to brush it off. "Doesn't that help him?"

"Of course," she said. "He might even regard it as a favor. But because of who you are, you don't have any standing."

I considered that for a moment. "You were there when I killed Draven. Would that give you standing in a meeting with this guy? Could you cling to my coattails?"

She arced her brow. "I am *not* clinging to your coattails."

"But I came up with the whole idea."

"And you could only execute it because I went in there all guns blazing," she said. "And because of Lockwood, who broke the window. If we hadn't been there, you would have died." She frowned. "But...you may have a point. Since Mill and I were both at that shindig where you killed Draven, and we were involved...yeah, we might be able to stake ourselves to your glory. No pun intended."

I smirked. "Next time, just own the pun. You know you want to."

"It might be cause to set up a parley," Iona said, ignoring my jest.

"Okay, let's say that you brought me instead of the other way around," I said.

"That's the only way this is gonna work," she said.

"I get that," I said. "But what would we say I was?"

"My slave?" She cringed.

"Nice try," I said.

"No, I'm quite serious."

I glared at her. "What, you mean like dragging me around with a chain on my neck?"

"Not so barbaric, no," she said. "But he would definitely have to believe that everything that has happened up to this point, including the issues with Draven, were because you were working for me."

"You'd be willing to take the blame for killing Theo? Because this is where all of this goes back to."

She considered it for a second. "Yeah, well, I sent you to that party in the first place, didn't I?"

I pursed my lips together. "Yeah. I guess you did. Still, how about instead of your slave, I can be your plus one?" Vampires were such savages, their barbarism chafed me.

"Nope," she said.

But she was smiling.

8

I knocked on a door that I had visited almost as much as Iona's. It was late, after eleven, and I was standing in a condo apartment, still sweating from the day's residual heat.

The door opened, and there he stood. Mill, with his dirty blond hair and gray-blue eyes. He smiled at me before leaning down to me, pressing his cool lips to mine as he drew me into his arms. I could have melted where I stood. And not just from the heat.

"Hi," he said softly, as we parted.

"Hey," I said, unable to keep my wit about me. "I can't stay long. Curfew and all."

"Fair enough," Mill said. "So, what's going on that you had to see me so late?" He sniffed, frowning deeply. "Wait...did you meet with the Oracle?"

"Wow," I said, sniffing myself. "You got that from smelling me?"

"Chewing gum, Swedish meatballs, and that IKEA furniture smell," Mill said, wrinkling his nose. "It's distinctive."

"Still...wow," I said. "Also, she's really not all that bad in spite of how you and Lockwood feel about her."

"Lockwood and I feel that way about her," Mill said patiently, "because she's crazy. Which we know because we've lived long enough to meet enough crazy people to judge."

I arched a brow at him. "She probably heard that, you know."

"Yes," he said. "Which does not take away from the fact she's crazy. But..." He sighed deeply. "I can see why you'd go to her. Surest place to get accurate information, I guess."

He was being awfully charitable. "Wait..." I said. "Do you know?"

His eyes danced with surprising mischief. "Know what?"

I cocked my head at him. "You already know everything, don't you? Sonofa..."

"There are no secrets in the vampire community, Cassie," Mill said. "Yeah. I know."

It was my turn to frown. "If you knew I was going to be attacked on the beach, why didn't you say something?"

His face went blank. "Okay, let me rephrase that...there was a secret in the vampire community before that happened. But after you killed half a dozen of Lord Varycas's vamps at the beach in broad daylight, it was not secret anymore, and thus it made its way to me." He looked me over. "Glad to see you're all right, by the way."

"Who told you?" I asked suspiciously.

He hesitated only a moment. "Lockwood. He came here as soon as it was over."

I must have made a 'scorned girlfriend' kind of noise, or maybe a 'betrayed friend' sort of sound. It was from deep within my throat, and I suspected if Lockwood had been here to hear it, he would have promptly gone invisible. Luckily, he wasn't, or he would have gotten an earful from me about tattling to my boyfriend. "So you know about Varycas, about Jacqueline–"

"Hold it," Mill said, holding up a hand. "Jacqueline? Your salty vampire friend from New York?"

"Yeah," I said. "She's the one who brought Varycas down on me."

Mill took a moment processing this. "Huh. That makes sense."

"Iona is in the process of contacting Varycas and setting up a parley right now," I said, then paused, frowning. "Is that really the right term? Are you guys like pirates or something?"

He shrugged. "It's an old word. Been used for centuries. We're creatures of habit and all that."

"This is why I like you. Whenever I encounter a word I'm curious about, you remember from when it was first used," I teased. "Sometime you're going to have to describe for me what the cavemen actually meant with those cave paintings, since you were there when they happened." Felt good to have something to rib him with, given how much he'd just surprised me with how much he knew.

"Still, a parley? Iona agreed to this?" he asked, ignoring my unsubtle dig at his age. "That surprises me."

"Well, she definitely didn't love the idea, but she saw that I had a point."

He ran his hands through his hair. "It's definitely an idea." He seemed to be trying very hard to be patient and just listen to me. Because the last time that we had this sort of conversation, it wasn't like this.

"Not exactly a ringing endorsement. Still..." I smiled at him. "...I appreciate the effort."

"Huh?" He blinked.

"You look like you're about to burst," I said. "Why don't you tell me what you're really thinking?"

He hesitated. It was clear that he didn't like the idea of starting another fight when things had been so okay between us for months now. "I...I'm just a little concerned, is all," he said slowly, deliberately. "I mean...do you remember what happened in Miami? I killed a vampire in his territory. That's an act of war to a vamp Lord. He almost certainly knows I did it, which will make any involvement for me...potentially uncomfortable. Put it this way – I'm already looking over my shoulder, knowing he's here."

"Great," I said. "I guess I'm relying on Iona to keep me safe in this."

"No, I'm still going," Mill said. "Besides, Iona's no guarantee of safety. Vampires operate under a distinct hierarchy: humans are cattle, Iona's like a peasant, and Varycas is the lord. If he wants to reach down and smite you, technically he can and there's not a lot she can do about it." The worried look on his face told me a lot.

"This just keeps getting better and better," I said, shaking my head.

"But," Mill added with a small smile. "Like I said, I'm all in. If this is what you want to do. But I'm nervous."

I pursed my lips thinly. "Do you see another way? Other than trying to clear the air?"

"I mean...you could kill Varycas and hope the next lord is less of a pain in the ass?" Mill said this with the straightest face, and it took me a moment to spot the gleam in his eye that told me he was kidding.

I laughed, and gave him an affectionate shove with my arm. "Because I'll definitely make it through that experience without injury again. Gah...I'd really like to just live my life without trying to challenge the millions of immortal, super-powerful creatures that share the planet with us–"

"Hundreds of millions," Mill amended. When my eyes widened, he shrugged. "Sorry. But it is. Which is why I agree with you. The last thing any of us wants is for the vampire world to be exposed. It'd mean war, which is a thing I can guarantee Varycas does not want. He'll want to keep this quiet. Whatever his plans are." He frowned. "Even the beach thing was a bit much for him, but I guess it was deniable enough for him to justify. Still...we should at least try and head this off. It's a whole lot better than trying to fight another lord." Any levity in his expression faded. "You were lucky to survive the last time relatively unscathed. I can almost guarantee that won't be the case if you try and face off with Varycas and his ilk."

"I hear you," I said. "And I agree. No more fighting." My phone vibrated in my back pocket, making me jump. I pulled it out, and saw Iona's name on the screen. I smirked. Apparently she had changed her contact photo when I wasn't paying attention. It was a picture of the two of us at the movies, all smiles. Which was still a weird look for Iona, IMO. "Hello?"

"Meeting is on," she said. "Like...now."

"Oh," I said, looking up at Mill. His brow furrowed, connecting like one, long, thick caterpillar. "Okay. That was fast."

"Varycas wants this settled before his official ascension," Iona said. "He's a proper British vampire Lord."

"Great, I want it settled, too," I said. Then my nerves kicked in and I asked, "...Is it a dinner meeting?"

"No," Iona said. "Tea. At the Don Cesar. Thirty minutes."

"Got it," I said. "We'll be there." And I hung up. Mill was waiting, tentatively, when I got off the phone, his face telling me, plainly, he had something to add. "What?" I asked. "Come on. Out with it."

He hesitated. "Isn't 'tea' what they call 'dinner' in England?"

I had a dinner meeting with the new vampire Lord of Tampa.

Well, crap.

9

"What...what even is this?" I asked, staring up at the Don Cesar building. "Pink? Really?"

The hotel was absolutely gorgeous, and located directly on the beach. It had to be one of the older buildings that I had seen in Florida, and that made it all the more impressive, making it stand out from all of the other typical hotels along the Gulf coast. And it was pink. Very pink. It looked a little like a palace, something straight out of a book.

"This better not be a grand waste of my time," Mill said.

"Because you have so much better things to do than meet your new ruler," Iona shot back.

"Varycas doesn't rule me."

"You should tell him that," Iona said. "Right to his face. Please. Just wait until I'm gone, because I enjoy my heart's current stake-free status."

"Let's just get this over with," I said.

Iona cocked her head, looking at me quizzically. "You mean the meeting? Or are you just trying to get us to stop arguing?"

"Honestly, both." I walked across the parking lot, which was quiet. No one would be on the beach at night, but there was a breeze coming off the water, rustling through my hair. The air was heavy with humidity, and the palm trees outside the hotel were waving in the wind. "It's almost eerie. Like...too quiet."

"I was thinking the same thing," Iona said.

There were greeters at the main entrance, dressed like bellhops from days long past. They smiled at us, opening the doors and bowing us through. I had stayed at nice places before, but what met us when we walked inside was a classic sort of luxury. The floors were long stretches of marble, and golden chandeliers hung from the ceiling, all lit and filling the room with warm light.

"Okay, so where are we meeting this guy?" I asked.

"Back terrace," Iona said. She seemed about fifty percent more tense than before we'd stepped inside. I guess even she was nervous about this dinner meeting even though she clearly wouldn't be dinner. Unlike some of us.

"Outside, good," I said. "I definitely am looking forward to this. So much."

Mill's face was hard, and he didn't reply.

Yes, this was my choice. Was this stupid? Probably. We made our way down a winding staircase, and followed signs to the pool area. The humidity spiked as we walked out onto the deck, back into the night air.

Lord Varycas was seated at a round table covered in a crisp white tablecloth, one leg crossed over the other, holding a teacup so properly that my grandmother would have been proud. His eyes found mine as I walked toward him, trying to fade into the background of my two vamp escorts. Still, I didn't want to look away like some prey animal, so I made eye contact and tried not to be too confrontational about it. He smiled between thin lips, and his eyes burned with an intelligence, and possibly a slyness, that I could not recall ever seeing from Draven.

Truly, he was the image of an old English Lord from the Victorian era. Nowhere near as physically imposing as Draven, in fact, though he was sitting I doubted he was all that much taller than me.

Another man stood off to the side dressed in all black. He was bald, and a silvery scar followed his jawline. Maybe it was the color, but I was immediately reminded of Lockwood's injuries; I wondered if it could have been caused by some sort of faerie magic? He watched us with burning animosity, though he said nothing.

Off to the other side of the Lord, leaning down to whisper in his ear, was a muscular female vampire, wide hipped with an electric pink mohawk that was buzzed on the sides. When she looked up, she was smirking.

Of course, the real show was the girl seated opposite the Lord, her arms folded over her chest, her thin face despoiled by a tightly clenched jaw, her dark eyes glaring daggers.

Jacquelyn.

Her dark hair was still tied in a tight, dark French braid that snaked over her shoulder and down her front. She had picked up a leather jacket along the way, and was wearing black skinny jeans with it. Guess it didn't matter if it was ninety-three degrees at night for vampires. She still looked cool.

"I don't like this," Mill said, staring out at the vampires on the terrace. "We should go."

I was about to agree with him when the Lord lifted his hand, and motioned us to join him. He wore that sly smile, and it unnerved me in ways I couldn't fully express. There was definitely something otherworldly about him, and I felt a visceral reaction. It was like my body knew, on sight, that this was a dangerous predator in spite of his outward appearance, and it was screaming, "Run! Run!"

His smile tried to put us at ease. It was saying, *Don't be shy. My bite isn't all that bad...*

"We're here now," Iona said, her eyes narrowing. "We might as well do what we came to. Stay behind me, Cassie. Let us do the talking."

"Because cattle can't speak," I muttered, but I did follow her over.

"Pay your respects to the Lord of Tampa," said the pink-haired woman. "You have come to meet with the great Lord Varycas, and you must act accordingly. Now...bow." She lowered her hands.

"Sorry," Mill said, his face hardening, "but like Barbie, I don't bend at the knees."

The look alone could have killed. Her mohawk quivered, and she gritted her teeth. "You are invited, and you disrespect your Lord?"

"That's quite enough, Jo," said Lord Varycas with a proper British accent. I was no expert, but he sounded like he'd just stepped out of Buckingham Palace. He held up a hand to silence her, holding his teacup and saucer with the other. "We are new in town, after all, and that's no way to treat our guests."

Apparently Jo didn't enjoy being told to shut up, but she obeyed, her narrowed eyes almost as resentful as Jacquelyn's.

"What a wonderful treat this is," Varycas said, placing his cup on the perfect white linen tablecloth, then straightened his lapels. "I'm so pleased you could join me here. Welcome to one of my favorite places in the entire world."

My eyes drifted to the teacup that he had just set down on the table.

The lip was coated in a thick, red liquid.

Never in my life had I seen wine cling to a cup quite like that.

10

"You'll have to excuse my entourage," Varycas said with a smile. His accent both put me at ease and set me on edge. The wind from the Gulf ruffled the tablecloth, as well as Jo's mohawk. "They are...very protective of me. And obviously big believers in the formalities of our society. Jo, Alfred," he nodded to the pink mohawk and then the bald, scarred man. "Kindly give our guests some...breathing room." Varycas smirked, looking right at me. It took me a second to realize that of all the people around this table, I was the only one actually breathing.

Varycas's gaze slid to Jacquelyn. "Have either of you made the acquaintance of my companion here? She's new in town as well, albeit not as new as I am."

"It's an honor to make your acquaintance," Iona said, strangely flat. She even inclined her head a little bit. I guess manners really did mean something to vampires. "My name is–"

Varycas smirked. "Oh, we all know who you are."

If Iona's face could have paled anymore, I think it would have.

"Your exploits have become quite the legend in Tampa." Varycas chuckled. "It isn't every day, after all, that a Lord as...prestigious and long-lived as Draven...bites the dust." A glint of amusement in his eyes gave away the game; he was thoroughly enjoying himself. "So...why don't you tell me why you've asked to meet with me? I'm curious what you hoped would come of this meeting."

Iona didn't glance at me. Right, I was cattle.

"We hoped to meet you and congratulate you on your rise to power in the Tampa territory," Iona said. "As vampires, we understand that no situation is going to be entirely perfect, but we certainly hope that we can come to some sort of peaceful agreement going forward that can suit everyone involved."

Varycas nodded as he listened. I watched for any sign of anger or dislike, but none came. In fact, it seemed as if he were genuinely pleased.

"The infighting in the territory has drawn the notice of witches and werewolves, always an inadvisable situation," Iona went on. "Thankfully, they never escalated to anything more than a few scuffles here and there–"

Scuffles? Was she serious? Almost dying as many times as I had only counted as *scuffles?*

"–and we have remained largely unnoticed by the growing population of humans in the Tampa area."

Jo rolled her eyes at the mention of the human population. Clearly, she had little regard for them.

There was a burning sensation in my cheek, and I glanced over to see Jacquelyn's sour face staring intently at me. She hadn't said a word, hadn't done anything. Was she waiting for Varycas to speak for her? That didn't seem like something she would do. She was more of a person who would stand up and fight her own battles.

So why was she here? What was her role? Why was Varycas humoring this newbie vampire who'd already led the previous Lord to ruin?

"I have heard all about the run ins with the accursed wolves," Varycas said. There was a sharp bite to his words. I guess he and Mill were on the same page in that regard. "I have also heard whispers of the Oracle's involvement?"

Iona hesitated. "No, sir. She has not gotten directly involved in the situations yet." As a liar, I recognized the weasel words there.

"Yet," he said, catching it as well. "Well, that's good to hear. The last time she became an active player in our world, there were months where I would have thought sunlight preferable to the existence I was living. I should like to see that era left safely in the past."

His gaze shifted to me for a brief moment before returning to Iona. He hadn't addressed me yet, not individually. Which was exactly what Iona had predicted.

"Draven was...not the easiest man to get along with," Iona said. "More interested in his parties than seeking peace for the vampires under his charge. We were hoping that things could be different with you. I'm sure that we aren't the only ones who have come to pay our respects to you and make our desires known."

"No, you are the first," Varycas said, swirling his teacup. "Though I'm sure that sensing the currents of power moving as they are," and here, he faintly smiled, "you shan't be the last." His eyes darted to me once more. "I do find it interesting that you've brought this one with you. And not as a peace offering, I assume?"

I stiffened as Iona said, "No. She's...with me."

"Indeed. Would you care to introduce her?" Varycas asked, smiling like he was enjoying every minute of this.

"She's...human," Iona said. She was straight as a ramrod.

"Oh, I'm well aware," Varycas said. "Still...let it not be said that our manners are not as superior as ourselves." And his smile slowly turned into a grin. "Come, now. Let's observe the little niceties, shall we?"

Iona and I exchanged a glance. She didn't betray any fear, and I hoped that my face was as steely as hers. "Of course," she said. "This is Cassie Howell...the human who helped to eliminate your predecessor."

The comment hung in the air, thick like fog. Alfred was as still as a statue. Jo's jaw was working, and she rolled her shoulders menacingly. Jaquelyn made no move, but she was a black hole of spite, sitting on the side of the table, hating me with her eyes.

And then Lord Varycas opened his mouth to speak.

"I know exactly who you are, Cassie Howell," Varycas said, smile growing wider on his face. "Of course. I could not have been more pleased when we were contacted about this meeting."

"Oh?" I said. "And why would you want to meet me?" My head was buzzing. I'd thought this meeting was a chance for Iona and Mill to lead the way while I sat in the background, letting the chauvinistic vampires speak among themselves to cut a deal on my behalf.

Instead, I was apparently the main event. Maybe this really was a dinner where I was to be the guest of honor. In the worst possible way.

Varycas laughed, doing nothing to put me at ease. "Why, to thank you, of course."

I blinked.

"You did me such a favor," he said. "A human defeating Draven? Why, that's madness. It's like a cow killing a human. Have you ever heard of such a thing?"

Mill cleared his throat. "Cows kill about twenty people a year." When everyone looked at him, he added. "That's more than sharks."

"Really?" Varycas seemed amused by this. "I would not have guessed that. But still, if it happens? It happens to ranchers and farmhands. You know, who actually work with them, hands on. Not to the people who really matter, you know?" That glint of amusement sparkled in his eye. "And I imagine it's not intentional. Not like what you did." He bared his teeth. "You became a stone cold vampire slayer. And look at you! Why you hardly look like the hardened, killing type."

"Um...thanks," I said. "I think?"

"You've become something of an urban legend," Varycas said. "Something to scare the fledglings with when they get out of line."

My cheeks flushed. "That's...just great."

"So," Varycas said, waving a hand in the air, "you are here to seek for peace, yes?" He eyed me with great amusement. "Your vampire slaying days are behind you now, and you wish to...what's that cowboy term? 'Ride off into the sunset?'" He chuckled. "Especially apropos for you, being as I imagine that stepping out your door at night these days would be quite...nerve-racking."

As if he was coming alive, Alfred moved toward another covered table along the wall, where a tea kettle was sitting on top of a small electric heating pad. With deliberate movements, he pulled the kettle off the heat.

"Uh...a little," I said. "Though after the beach incident today, I'm starting to see that the sun is not necessarily a guarantee of protection."

"Very wise," Varycas said, as Alfred brought the kettle back over to the table, and stooped over Varycas's teacup. He refilled it with the thick, red liquid that was steaming. "That was a message, you see? I may be grateful that you opened this territory to my influence, but I can't have you out there thinking that you're the Lord of Tampa now." His toothy grin revealed those pointy teeth vamps were famous for. "Or whatever you prefer to call yourself. 'The Great Cow of Tampa.'" He laughed, and his entourage did, too. "There is an order to things, you see, and when things become out of order...action must be taken."

Bile rose in my mouth as the smell hit me. Sharp and metallic, it was all I could do not to gag. The teacup, I realized, as I tried to hide the sick feeling rising in my throat.

"So, you want peace? Fair enough. What terms do you propose?" Varycas asked, lifting the freshly filled cup to his lips once more. I had to clasp my hands behind my back to keep them from shaking out of revulsion. He smiled pleasantly up at me as he set his teacup back down.

"I want the vampires to leave me, my family, and my friends out of...whatever it is that happens," I said. "I want us to be left alone. Like none of this ever even happened. Like we don't exist in your world."

Varycas smiled. "Of course. We didn't invite you into our world. You were dragged in by a vampire with...peculiar interests. As to your proposal...absolutely. We want peace. Peace is in everyone's best interest. A return to status quo ante, before any of this." His grin got toothier. "A chance for your legend to fade, and your life to return to...ah...normal. For a human, anyhow. I consider this entirely reasonable. And absolutely possible."

There was such a lightness in his tone that I was caught off guard. "You...really mean that?" I asked.

"Why would I not?" he asked. "War is a terrible start to a new Lord's agenda, especially when the last one managed to get all of his subjects killed over such insignificant feuds. Very well. Peace we want, and peace we shall have." He stood, putting down his teacup and buttoning his jacket. "Let today at the beach be the last of the death dealt between us."

Hope washed over me like a tidal wave. "Wait...are you serious?"

"Of course," he said. "My people have little interest in war with your kind, especially on behalf of an already dead Lord who I have no loyalty to." He shrugged. "We can reach an arrangement to put this all behind us."

Wasn't it weird that he wasn't treating me like cattle as Iona and Mill had expected? Here he was, speaking to me like I was...an equal. I didn't want to look to either of them for guidance, and thus prove Varycas's point about me being a cow subject to their superiority, but I was curious what they thought.

"However..." Varycas said.

My eyes moved back to him. Uh oh. There was the other shoe.

"If I am agreeing to leave your people alone, then you will have to agree to leave my vampires alone."

Was that it? I nodded. "All right. I can manage that."

His smile darkened slightly. "Let us be entirely clear. You see...humans will die. That's only natural. It happened under Draven's rule, and it will happen under mine."

"Now, wait a second," I said. "I never agreed to–"

"It's part of living in a vampire's territory," he said. His tone was so casual it was as if he were discussing the winnings of a golf tournament. "Humans kill cows for food, yes? But there are still plenty of them. I promise that we will not cull the entire population. Not even anywhere close."

I frowned. The cow analogy was really starting to get on my nerves.

Jacquelyn's face twisted into a wicked grin, and one of her brows arched. She was enjoying this way too much.

"You don't have to worry," he said. "We'll keep it quiet. We'll keep the numbers...manageable. It won't look like a war. It will be peace and calm," Varycas said, almost merrily. "But you have to stay out of vampire affairs."

These people who would die...would it be my fault?

"This is the deal," Varycas said. "Vampires and humans have lived in peace for hundreds of years. All that time, this was happening, and your people never saw it. I offer you that same return to normalcy. A chance to...get your life back." He smiled.

No. I wouldn't be involved. He was going to do it whether I tried to attack him right then and there or I didn't. This was part of living in a vampire's territory? That didn't mean I had to like it.

But in the name of peace...

"Do we have deal?" Varycas asked. He took another sip from his cup.

I swallowed my fears, hoping that his next full kettle didn't come from someone I knew.

What could I do, anyway? I may have taken on the last vampire Lord, but he'd been overconfident. As unaware, in his way, of what humans were capable of as I'd been of what vamps could do before I met Byron. For months I'd fought them and worried and failed and lived in terror that something awful was going to happen to someone I cared about.

Now...it could all be over. And all I had to do was close my eyes and not see what had been going on for longer than I'd even been alive.

"Yes," I said.

"Wonderful," he replied. He stood to his feet, and offered his outstretched hand to me.

I took it and we shook, his frigid palm against my slick, sweating, warm one.

Jacquelyn and Jo were both seething out of the corner of my eye, but Varycas was all smiles. Out of the corner of my eye, Iona wore a tight smile, while Mill was practically expressionless. A veritable bevy of reactions.

As for me? I felt a cold, gripping feeling deep in my stomach, relief mixed with worry that I couldn't define. It was over, after all, and I could get back to just living my life like a normal teenage girl.

Shouldn't I have been happy?

11

"I could have done without the steaming teacup of blood," I admitted once we were back in the car, rolling through the quiet streets on the way home. Who was out past her curfew? This girl.

Mill, who was in the back seat, chuckled. "You lost all your color when Alfred brought him his fresh cup," he said. "I wondered if I was going to have to carry you out of there."

"That did not go how I expected..." Iona said. "For one, I'm amazed that he acknowledged you at all." She glanced over at me. "Given his reputation, I thought he'd just ignore you."

"I guess you made a bigger splash in the vampire world than we thought," Mill said.

"But was he telling the truth?" I asked. "About peace, I mean."

Iona's face hardened. "I don't know. You tell us."

I stared out of the window again. The big, white dome of Tropicana stadium came into view, all of the bright white lights making it look like an enormous balloon in the darkness.

"That's the thing," I said. "I didn't get a lying vibe from him. At all. If anything, like you, I'm genuinely surprised that he even deigned to speak to me."

"He seemed interested in what happened between you and Draven," Mill said.

"I think he respects you," Iona said.

"I don't know if I would go that far," I said.

"Why not? He was speaking to you like an equal. And you're a human. You're as good as–"

"I know, cattle, I got it," I said. "Speaking of the vampires taking out humans...I have to admit that I'm really not all that comfortable with the idea that he could just send his cronies out there to kill some random people."

"Well, he agreed to leave your family and friends alone, right?" Mill said.

"Yeah, but that doesn't mean I'm not worried about the rest of the human population in Tampa," I said.

"Before you came to Tampa, the vampires were doing what vampires do," Mill said. "Like Varycas said, it happens in every territory. Vampires need blood to survive. And as you know, not every vampire is nice and friendly and ethically sources from a blood bank."

"I know that your people have been murdering and eating us for millennia," I said, way more calm than such a statement deserved, "but that doesn't mean I have to like it."

"You don't have to feel guilty about people who might get hurt," Iona said. "The whole world isn't your responsibility, Cassie."

"I'm aware of that," I said.

"And most vampires tend to go after criminals, or people who might not be quite so wholesome," Iona said.

"Well, not always," Mill said. "Sometimes they go after

that poor unfortunate soul who was out too late, stumbling home drunk after a hard day, and–"

The glare that Iona shot Mill shut him up immediately.

I frowned, and sighed heavily. "I just don't know how I am going to handle it the first time I hear on the news that some poor little girl has gone missing. I'll know exactly the reason why, and it is going to take a lot of self control not to march into Varycas's...wherever he lives, and give him a piece of my mind. Or possibly a stick of wood to the heart."

"Most of the time, you aren't going to hear anything," Mill said. "Unless someone really screws up."

My stomach clenched painfully. I was not appreciating how flippantly he was discussing this.

"Just...don't worry about it, okay?" Iona said. She was using her best soothing tone that she reserved for me when she wanted to play big sister. "Because here's the thing... more people are going to die if you decide to have a vampire war."

"Yeah, and we all saw how that went," I said.

"No, you didn't," Iona said. "You have no idea what a real vampire war would be like. What Draven did was nothing. Modern society is unprepared for the brutality of vampires – age-old vampires, who lived in the days when a pogrom was a standard operating procedure – unleashing them- selves. You really don't want to see what that would be like."

I swallowed nervously.

"But..." she said. "I don't think that's anything we need to worry about. We leave them alone, they'll leave us alone. Everybody ends up happy, right?"

The hope started to come back to me.

"You're right," I said.

I stared back out of the window as we started over the long stretch of the bay toward Tampa. I was hopeful.

Peace. Was it possible that after everything I had been through with Byron, and Draven, and the werewolves...that it could all just...end?

Wasn't that what I had wanted the whole time? Isn't it what I was hoping for all along?

As I watched the lights of Tampa ahead, for the first time since this afternoon on the beach, I started to entertain the possibility that yes, my life could settle back down to that of a normal high school girl.

12

"Oh my gosh, girl. You look *so* cute."

"You really think so?"

I was standing just inside the door to my bedroom, Xandra and Laura waiting just out in the hall, pronouncing their approval after I opened the door.

"See, I knew the dark teal would go nice with your hair," Xandra said with a smile. "And you wanted to get the black." She sniffed. "What's the perfume?"

"Black looks better for formal wear," I said. "At least, it usually does. And I don't know on the scent. Someone gave it to me, but it lacks a label." I wrinkled my nose. "Kinda smells of generic roses?"

"Mm, roses. So you agree that I made the right call?"

I rolled my eyes. "Yes, yes. You made the right call."

"But seriously, it really brings out the color of your eyes," Laura said. "Makes them really pop." She emphasized her point by making her hands pop open like fireworks in front of her face. "Mill is going to love it."

"Thanks, guys," I said.

Laura's sleeveless dress was silver, covered in sequins,

and fell all the way to the floor, with a simple beaded detail around her waist, and her hair was in a neat bun at the nape of her neck.

Xandra was the opposite. She was wearing a fire engine red dress that fell to her knees, but the skirt was made of several layers, which made it almost poofy. Her hair, which was more blue than purple at the moment, was down and curled with thick ringlets. Movement down the hall caught my eye, and I stared past them.

Iona had arrived. And...wow.

I always knew that Iona was pretty, but tonight she looked like a knockout. She wore black high heels that could easily be used as stakes, and wore a black dress that fell just above the knees. I'd never seen her in a sleeveless anything, and something was different about her face–

"You wore makeup," I said, as the realization dawned on me. "You look great!"

"Iona!" Laura exclaimed. "You look amazing!"

"Thanks," she said. "Blue suits you."

I grinned. "Yeah, well, Xandra – "

"Talked her into it," Xandra said with a grin. "Sure did."

"Finally got your cast off, I see," Iona said. She was looking down at Xandra's bare arm.

"Yep, a few days ago," Xandra said. "Couldn't wait to, either. The sweating and the itchiness were driving me insane. I really wanted to get it off before tonight." She'd had it on for weeks, ever since the beach incident. And had been grousing about it the whole time.

"Cassie, the boys are here." Mom's voice echoed down the hall.

I glanced at myself one last time in the bathroom mirror. My makeup was done, though I hadn't caked it on. Just some blush, eyeshadow and liner, and a pale pink lipstick. I hoped that Mill would like the color. And all of my curls were behaving so far. I had half my hair pinned up in a barrette that I had borrowed from Iona. Satisfied, I left the mirror behind and joined the others.

"I just can't believe school is starting again on Wednesday," Laura said, frowning. "This summer went way too fast."

"Well, we live in Florida, so technically it's summer all year round," Xandra said. "Actually, we do have four seasons. 'Hot,' 'really hot,' 'hurricanes,' and then 'actually pretty nice.' But that one only lasts like two days."

Laura's eyes brightened as she looked up at me. "This was a great idea, though, Cassie. I'm so glad you thought of it. What a fun way to say goodbye to summer."

I grinned at her. Since my brain wasn't consumed with thoughts of protecting my friends and family from vampire attacks any longer, I found I had a lot more time on my hands. It had been a really fun summer, aside from that one day at the beach and the awkward encounter with the overly friendly Lord Varycas.

Still, since then, it had been quiet, and the longer it was quiet, the more I believed that Varycas had been telling the truth. Peace was going to be upheld as long as I kept my nose out of his business.

The more I distanced myself from that world, the more I wanted to make sure it stayed that way. I was starting to crave the quiet and serenity that I was having on a daily basis. Things that would have at one point annoyed me, like the dog across the street barking at two in the morning, or having to stand in line behind the person with the super full grocery cart in the ten items or less lane no longer did. I was content to just live life, and to share it with those around me.

Okay, to be brutally honest, the ten items or less thing

still got to me. But I was trying to be better. More...peaceful. But they could help by, y'know, standing in any of the other checkout lines with their full cart.

Mom and Dad had noticed the change. They weren't happy when I told them that I had gone to meet with the new vampire Lord. They understood why I'd done it, though, and I think now that things had returned to normal, they'd come to a point where they were thankful I had.

Sure, there were still nights when I woke in a cold sweat, gasping for breath, terrified because I imagined Draven's sneering face standing right over me, or sensing Byron's presence against the skin of my neck. All things considered, though, I was learning how to live with those memories, how to push them aside and keep them away.

We found Mom and Dad and the guys out in the living room, standing just inside the kitchen. The boys – Gregory, Derrick, and Mill – were all dressed up in suits. It was all part of the event planned for tonight, this last, sentimental goodbye to what was probably the best summer of my life. I had friends, we had fun, and I'd kicked lying out of my life.

"Wow, you're wearing a tie?" Xandra asked, grabbing Gregory's green tie and giving it a tug. "Did your mom have to knot it for you?"

Gregory blushed, and snatched the tie out of her hand. "Of course not."

"Got it. Dad did," she said.

"No, it's called a single Windsor, and it's surprisingly easy to execute."

"You look beautiful."

I looked up to see Mill standing in front of me. His suit was a charcoal grey, with a pressed white shirt and a navy blue tie.

My heart skipped a few beats.

"Yeah, you don't look so bad yourself," I said. He stole a quick kiss on my cheek before Mom came up to me. She had that look in her eye, like she was holding in tears of pride.

"Oh, Cassie, I love how you put your hair up like that," she said. She came over and did the mom thing, fussing with me.

"Mom," I said. "It's fine, I like it the way it is."

She smiled at me. Then she turned to everyone else. "All right! Let's go get some pictures out on the lawn! You all look so beautiful! And so handsome!"

Xandra gave me a sarcastic sort of smile as she followed my mom out. "You'd think we were going to prom," she whispered to me. "Like, nerd prom."

"I mean, it's kind of like prom," Laura said, overhearing her. "We're going to a really nice event, and there will be food at a yummy place afterward."

Her eyes widened. "Are there steaks at this yummy place?"

I laughed. "Definitely. But only if you feel like spending forty bucks."

Laura's face paled. "Oh. Maybe not, then. Are there kale salads?"

Mom lined us all up in front of the hedges out in front of the house, where she and Dad proceeded to snap a million pictures of us until we started to complain that our faces hurt from smiling so much. "Now, what's the name of the show that you are going to see again?" Dad asked as we made our way back inside so the girls could collect their shawls and purses.

Lockwood had just pulled up in a black stretch limo he'd rented just for the occasion. It looked like a black hole of pure luxury as it slid into place at the street, waiting to whisk us away for our magical eve. Which would not, hopefully, include any actual magic usage.

It really was like prom.

"*Into the Woods*," I said.

"And it's at which theater?"

"The Royal Crown," I said. "I should be getting out around eight. Then we're going to the restaurant, which is only a ten-minute walk from the theater." I glanced over at Iona's heels, then at Xandra's, which were nearly as tall. Maybe I should reconsider the walking plan.

"Okay, good," Dad said. "What time do you think you'll be home?"

"I don't know, eleven?" I said.

"That's perfect," Dad said. "All right, does everyone have everything? Their phones that are hopefully fully charged so your parents can get in touch with you?" He smiled tightly. "You know how we worry."

"Oh, Xandra, sweetie, can I have your mom's new cell phone number? I forgot to ask her for it the last time I saw her, and I want to send her some of these pictures," I heard Mom say.

Xandra rattled it off as Gregory sidled over to Laura, who was reapplying some lipstick by using the selfie mode on her phone's camera.

"I think you look...really nice," Gregory mumbled.

Laura looked at him, her cheeks turning pink. "Um...you too," she said.

I rolled my eyes as Dad turned away. He seemed to be reddening as well, watching these kids.

"Everybody ready?" Mill called from the door.

Everyone apparently was ready, because they all started toward the door.

"Cassie, do you have your phone charged, too?" Dad asked.

"Oh, my phone," I said. "Hold on, guys, I'll be right with you. Just have to go grab my purse."

I hurried back to my room, grateful that I hadn't chosen heels like Xandra suggested, and snatched the formal purse I'd packed just for this occasion off my bed. Opening it up, I found my wallet, my keys, my phone, and my ticket for the play.

I hesitated. A feeling anchored me in place, like I had lead in my feet. I was forgetting something. What was it? I glanced around, and my eyes fell on the surface of the dresser.

Resting on top of it was a slender piece of wood. It was tipped with iron, specially made to slay both vampires and fairies. It had been a long time since I had had to use it. A whole summer, in fact.

But that hadn't meant that I had broken the habit of carrying it on me.

"Just in case..." I murmured as I slid it into my purse.

It was like carrying mace or a pocketknife. Only I knew that the real enemy to humans were vampires. Maybe twenty years from now I'd stop carrying it, if this peace held. But for now, it was still too much of a habit.

"Be careful," Mom said. She passed me my silver shawl that I had borrowed from her just in case it was too cold in the theater. It wasn't like Mill's room temp arm around me was going to help. "And call us if you need us."

"I will," I said. I gave her a swift hug, then gave one to Dad, too.

"And have fun," Dad said. "You did a great job planning this night for your friends. I think it was a great idea."

I smiled. "Should be fun." Before things could get any

sappier, I said goodbye, and headed outside. I found Iona waiting just outside the door. She was nearly dancing on the balls of her feet. I don't know quite how she achieved that in those heels, but she looked both antsy and pleased. "Everyone already in the limo?" I asked.

"Yep."

I looked at her, and grinned. "You're positively glowing with excitement."

She glowered, stopping her twitching. "I am not," she said, back to her cool self. "I would so much rather be home watching a movie than hanging out with all these losers."

But I just smiled. Then why would she have clearly put so much effort into looking great tonight? Still, I allowed her that tiny self-delusion, that little lie. We climbed into the limo, my cheeks burning from smiling so much.

"Are we ready?" Lockwood asked, from beyond the divider window. Well, wasn't that a nostalgic sight, seeing him in his driver's outfit, ready to chauffeur me somewhere nice?

"Definitely," I said.

And off we went, the excitement of the night so thick we could have cut it with a spoon.

13

———

The curtains closed to thunderous applause and the lights in the theater rose once more. I blinked against the brightness as the attendees rose to their feet and started toward the exits, a chatter filling the The Royal Crown theater and jarring me out of my stupor.

"Wow," Gregory said, a few seats down. "That was really good! I didn't know what to expect coming in."

"Yeah, it was way better than the movie," Laura said as she got to her feet. Stretched her arms up over her head, her dress shimmered.

I turned to Mill, the low buzz of a thousand conversations going on around us. "What did you think?"

He hesitated before answering. "I've seen it a few times."

"But wasn't it good?" I asked.

"Yeah, it was good," he said. But there was a reluctance to his tone.

"You've seen it on Broadway, haven't you?" I asked.

Mill stiffened, then smiled. "I didn't want to disappoint you."

I rolled my eyes. My worldly boyfriend. It was going to

be tough to find a new experience we could share together. Other than maybe Fortnite.

"Guys, I'm starving," Derrick said, grabbing his stomach. Overly dramatic much?

"Me too, bro," Gregory said. "Hey, Cassie, when are we getting food?"

"Now, if you don't plan on sitting here all day," I said. I turned and urged Iona down the row. The seats were just tight enough together that we all had to go sideways, even though they were empty. Why they packed theater seating so tightly was beyond me. I followed her down the row to the plush, carpeted aisle. We filed into the line of people making their way out of the theater. Behind me, I could hear snatches of discussion about the play from Xandra and Laura.

"–Interesting take on fairy tales–" Laura said.

"–couldn't believe they just killed him like that–" Xandra said.

"What did you think, Cassie?" Iona was looking over her shoulder at me as we moved from the theater into the lobby. The ceiling was decorated to look like an old Roman building, with tall pillars and detailing in the arched beams. Chandeliers with fake candles hung above us.

"I really liked it," I said. The lobby was packed, voices filling the cavernous space. I kept looking over my shoulder to make sure the group was together, not wanting anyone to get lost in the crowd as we fought our way toward the front entrance. The air grew stuffy, and the humidity was high outdoors, giving no relief to the stifling lobby with its doors thrown wide, the air conditioning unable to keep up with the sheer number of bodies in the space. When we finally broke free onto the sidewalk, the air was just as heavy, and there was no breath of fresh air to be had. It was like breathing warm soup.

"How are there just as many people out here as there are inside?" Gregory asked, staring around as he and the others came to a halt beside me. He adjusted his glasses with his knuckle and stared around. "And it's even hotter out here." He mopped his brow. "Okay, what are we doing?"

"Walking to the restaurant." I pulled my phone from my purse and turned on the screen. There were two texts waiting from Lockwood. One asking if the play was finished, and the other to let me know that he was waiting for us at the restaurant, and our table was ready.

"Awesome," I said. "Lockwood has our table. Anyone want me to have him order some drinks for us?"

"Ooh, Sprite for me, please," Laura said.

"I'll take a sweet tea," Xandra said.

"Dr. Pepper," said Derrick.

Gregory's face screwed up in concentration. "Um...water – no, lemonade. No, I changed my mind. I want chocolate milk." Derrick shot him an amused look. "I like what I like. Don't judge," Gregory said.

I texted Lockwood our drink orders, and looked at Iona and Mill. "Anything for you guys?"

"I packed us a few things," Mill said. "Lockwood should have them already."

I nodded. Got it. Didn't need to know more than that. That settled, I opened up the maps app. The GPS located us, and the restaurant was the most recent search. "Okay, it's not a long walk from here. Only about ten minutes that way."

Xandra glared at me. "You didn't tell me we'd be walking for ten minutes. I have heels on."

"Oh, and you were just telling me how you were getting the hang of it," Laura said, a little pityingly.

"Yeah, 'getting the hang of it' doesn't mean that I'm a master," Xandra said. Then she stumbled.

"Come on," I said, and started up the sidewalk.

The crowds were thick, making it hard to move more than a few feet at a time without having to say "Excuse me," every few seconds. I heard the others echoing it behind me as we tried to head west. Ten minutes my butt. With this many people, we were going to get there just before they closed.

Moving through the incessant crowds with the warm evening air close around us, suddenly the little hairs on the back of my neck stood up. I froze, looking around.

Xandra bumped into me, then Gregory into her. I managed to keep from toppling over like a row of dominoes, but only just. "Hey, why'd you stop?" Xandra asked, wobbling on those heels.

But I was staring around.

Eyes at a small bistro table in the shadows were staring at me.

Eyes just outside the doors to the theater were staring at me.

The eyes of the guy standing next to the parking meter were staring at me.

Vampire, vampire, vampire.

"Um, Mill?"

"I see it. I see them," he said.

"Iona?"

"Yep," she said. "That's...a lot."

My throat went dry.

"What? What is it?" Xandra asked.

"I don't know if we can fight this many," I said. Another three across the street. Two more farther up the sidewalk, walking slowly toward us, against the onrushing theater crowd. Who knew how many we couldn't actually see.

"Fight? What do you mean?" Xandra was right there, at my shoulder, and I could hear the hesitation in her words.

"Fight," I said softly. Because...

...We were surrounded.

14

"What are they doing here?" I asked.

"Don't know," Iona said. "But they sure don't look happy, do they?"

"Do vamps ever look happy?" Xandra asked. "I mean, other than over a fresh pint of O neg?"

"Are they part of Varycas's clan?" I asked.

"Hard to say," Mill said, looking around. With each sweep of his gaze, my trepidation grew that much more. "This is his territory, though. Hard to imagine someone else would send a war force in of this size without his knowledge, at least."

"What are you talking about?" Xandra asked. She had grabbed onto my arm and was shaking it. "You don't mean–"

"Shut up," I whispered. It was a bad idea to say the word *vampire* out in the open like that. Especially with so many of them watching.

But that was all they were doing. Watching. Intently, sure, but that was all. None of them had so much as made a move toward us in the last thirty seconds. Even the two who'd been cutting through the crowd up the sidewalk had just stopped in their tracks and were lingering ahead. "What are they planning?" I asked.

"Your guess is as good as mine," Iona said. "How far is the restaurant from here?"

"A few blocks," I said.

"All right, let's move," Iona said, getting ahead of me and heading through the dense crowd.

"Wait," I said. "This is crazy. What if they're here to start trouble? All of these people around..."

"Then we definitely shouldn't be here," Mill said. "We're way too exposed. Let's just keep walking."

"What's the matter?" Laura asked, appearing around perhaps the tallest man I had ever seen. Gregory and Derrick were close behind her. They caught one look at the expression on my face before starting to assault me with questions.

"What's the matter?"

"What happened?"

"Why do you look so upset?"

Iona gave me a warning look, but I ignored it. They had to know. If this was going to turn into a battle, then they had to be aware before it happened. Dropping my voice, I waved them in closer to me. "Vampires," I said just loud enough for them to hear me. "They're pretty much everywhere – no, Gregory, don't look. Not right now."

"We have to get out of here," Laura said, her perfectly manicured eyebrows now two dashes of surprise.

"Yeah, but how?" Gregory asked. "If they are everywhere, how are we going to leave?"

"Where's Lockwood?" Derrick asked, gaze was hard and concerned. He'd lost a lot of the color in his cheeks.

"At the restaurant already, remember?" I said.

"We need to move," Mill said a little more firmly from behind me.

"I agree," Derrick said. "Let's just stick to the plan, and hope they just...let us go?"

"We have no guarantee that they are here for us, right?" Xandra asked. "I mean, it's been so quiet for so long. Why all of the sudden–"

I wanted to believe she was right with every fiber of my being. But there was a nagging doubt at the back of my mind. My palms were slick with sweat, and my heart was racing. "We don't know if they're here for us," I said. "But we don't want to stick around and find out, do we?"

"Can we call for an Uber?" Laura asked.

"Let's sit here on the sidewalk and wait for an Uber while vampires come eat us," Gregory said. "Good plan."

Someone in the crowd laughed out loud like a hyena, and we all jumped. It was too much like a scream. The shadows seemed darker all of the sudden. The lights out in front of the theater weren't bright enough.

Damn. Why had I let my guard down?

But at the same time, how could I have known that there would be a whole pack of vampires outside the theater waiting?

Waiting for what, though?

"Cassie," Iona said, more firmly. She took my hand in hers, and it was so cold. "Let's get moving."

I could feel the eyes of the vampires on the back of my head as I turned toward Mill. They easily outnumbered us, and there were tons of people around. Real people, humans. I checked the map on my phone again; the restaurant was minutes away.

If we were to walk slowly and surely, using the dense crowd around us as cover, maybe we wouldn't have to worry about the vampires coming after us at all. Varycas had said that vampires were going to hunt in Tampa. But would he allow them to do so out in the open like this?

None of the civilians seemed to notice the threat. The theater goers were happy and carrying on, and their jubilation was making me wince. If the vamps were going to attack, they would have attacked by now, right? Wouldn't they have grabbed us as soon as we were out of the theater? Total ambush?

Regardless, we needed to move. Iona and Mill hung back, letting me take the lead as we walked away from the theater. The others fell into step silently behind me, their eyes roaming all over the sidewalk crowds, looking for more eyes rooted on us. All of the excitement and joy of the evening had been robbed from us, and I hoped that the further away we got, the danger might subside, and we could all breathe a sigh of relief.

But it seemed a lot more likely to me that they were going to lurk, and follow, and that somehow, after all these months of peace, I was about to finish my evening at an impromptu vampire dinner party after all.

15

A scream split the hot, humid night, cutting through the shimmering air. A real scream, this time. That of a woman, coming from somewhere back near the theater. It pierced the evening, shrill and terrifying. It acted as a trigger that rang over the crowd, spooking the herd. Seconds later, when another echoed down the street, it set off the stampede.

Then the running started. And the shouting, and the shoving. People pushed aside their own friends and loved ones to get out of the way of whatever was coming at them.

My heart plummeted. The vampires...were attacking the crowd.

"Run!"

It was Iona, and she was shoving her way along the side-walk. It was hard to hear her over the din. People were jumping over tables, knocking over chairs at the outdoor seating of nearby restaurants. Horns honked as people rushed into the street. Others shoved their way back inside the theater, or into storefronts.

"What are they doing?" Derrick called.

"Heading this way," Mill said. "Move!"

"Wait, they're coming after us?" Laura asked, all the color draining from her face. "Right here?"

"Looks like it," Mill said. His brow was furrowed, and he turned, already in his fighting stance.

He was right. There were easily a dozen of them, stalking toward us, teeth bared, smiles curling up their faces like they were going to enjoy what was coming. My stomach turned over when I saw the bodies of people lying on the sidewalk, and I didn't know if it was the shadows or blood from their injuries that were causing the darkness pooled beneath them.

"Mill, we can't fight them," I said. "There's too many."

"Do you have a better idea?" he asked as a group of people ran past, shrieking hysterically.

"Wait a second, I thought we had peace with these guys," Gregory said. "There was supposed to be peace. Where is this peace?"

"Not in evidence, obviously," Mill said.

"Get inside!" Xandra cried. "Get off the streets! Get the hell away from here!" She was standing beside the door to one of the restaurants, waving people inside. It deeply moved me. We had to get away and she was doing what she could to help innocent people get to safety.

"Xandra, come on," I said, reaching out and grabbing her hand. "They'll be safe after we get out of here." Laura fumbled around with something in her purse as the crowds kept pushing passed us. "What are you doing?" I asked.

She withdrew a thin piece of wood, sharpened at the end. A stake. "Never leave home without it," she said.

"Neither do I," Xandra said, producing one of her own from her purse.

I yanked mine out and looked around.

Mill and Iona had pushed through the crowd enough and had started engaging the two vamps out front. Iona clocked one in the side of the jaw before he realized what was coming, and Mill doused the other with a vial of holy water that he had pulled from somewhere.

"Get to Lockwood!" came Iona's voice as she ducked beneath the punch of another vamp. This one had crossed the street to attack. The crowd had started to thin; most had dispersed either back into the theater or into the restaurants and bars up and down the street. The insanity was dying down, leaving us with a steadily growing number of vampires coming toward us from behind.

"We'll hold them off for as long as we can!" Mill added, waving frantically up the street.

"Come on, Cassie, let's run," Laura said. She yanked her high heeled shoes off of her feet and tossed them aside. Xandra did the same, but held onto hers.

I kicked mine off as well. "Let's go," I said, and I dashed down the street between Iona and Mill, heading for the restaurant ahead and hoping we'd all make it – together.

16

Every snarl I heard sent a spike of fear through my heart, catching my breath in my throat as I ran down the lamplit street. Was it right behind me? Was it about to catch me, or sink its teeth into someone I cared about?

Frequent glances back as I pounded, barefoot, down the concrete road, dress trailing behind me, revealed that Mill and Iona were doing a decent job at keeping the vampires off our backs. They were bringing up the rear, my friends strung out over about twenty feet, each of us adapting our running speed to the group.

Behind, the vampires closed, lurking a little ways back, like sharks circling just beyond an aquarium wall. As we ran, the traffic from the road beside us whizzed by, unaffected by either our plight or the panic outside the theater. I kept glancing down at my phone, my lifeline, the only source of salvation that we could find.

"Only seven minutes from here, guys," I called.

"Seven?" Gregory said. "Oh, come on, you couldn't have picked some place closer?"

"Like I knew that we were going to get attacked by vampires!"

"Well, you should have," Gregory said. "This is you we're talking about, after all."

Wow, Gregory. Thanks for the vote of confidence. Exactly what I needed right now. But I knew he was desperate too. Desperate to escape, to be out of their grip. All of us were. And as much as I hated to admit it, he was right. This always led back to me.

Our only hope was to reach Lockwood and the restaurant. When we did, we could hop in the limo and escape. It was the only thing that was going to be able to save us at this point. We couldn't outrun them. Not all the way home. They would overtake us in a minute. Fresh, hot fear pulsed through me, making my stomach turn over.

Every second that passed put us closer to the restaurant, closer to freedom.

I could hear the others panting as our feet pounded the sidewalk. People who had heard the screaming from the theater were standing out on the sidewalk, standing on their tiptoes, trying to catch a glimpse of whatever had happened. They leapt out of the way in surprise as we ran past. Some cried out to us, asking if we needed help or if we knew what was going on.

I knew we would be putting them in danger if we stopped running. Not to mention there was nothing they could do to protect or help us. And I didn't have the breath in my lungs to shout a reply.

Motion out of the corner of my eye made me turn my head; Mill was there, with a fresh scratch on his cheek. He moved with blurry speed, meeting my eyes for a second, then turning back, looping behind us. The vampires were moving in, hard and fast on our tails.

"There's too many of them," Laura said. Her breathing was hard and fast as she got ahead of me. All of that cheerleading had paid off; she was probably in better shape than the rest of us.

"What do we do?" Derrick said. "We can't fight this many. If they catch us–"

"They won't catch us if we keep moving," I said. I hoped; there was very little concrete reason for me to believe that. They were insanely fast and strong, and we were normal people. The crowd that we'd left behind had not slowed them down nearly enough.

I heard a scream behind me, and with a jolt, I chanced a glance over my shoulder. Iona had just run up the wall of the building beside us like some kind of superhero before throwing herself on top of one of the vampires that was quickly gaining on us. She landed on the vamp and drove a stake through its heart. It fell to the ground, gurgling as it dissolved into a black pile of goo.

Mill, behind her, was keeping the rear guard, swatting at any that came too close, his fingers covered in slimy, black vampire blood. My stomach felt like it was in my throat as I watched the oily goo drip onto the sidewalk. My mouth was dry as I panted for air, and a stitch had formed in my side. It would be so easy to give up, to just stop running. It hurt. It hurt so badly.

But the fear kept moving me forward. My heart would probably stop working before my body decided to give up. "We have to get to the restaurant," I said. "Lockwood is there. He's the only one with the way to get us out of here. We can't run; there's too many. But if we get a car, and a faerie, we might be able to escape."

"You think so?" Gregory repeated, more loudly, more fearfully.

"I don't know, okay?" I snapped. "Just...give me a second to think."

"We don't have a second," Xandra said. The worry in her voice was making me even more anxious.

"Let's turn up here," Derrick suggested as we approached the mouth of an alley. A glance back showed the vamps had retreated slightly. Maybe Iona and Mill's counterattacks had put the fear in them. "Maybe we can find some way to lose them."

"We need to get to the restaurant," Laura said. "That's the only priority."

I glanced at my phone again. "No, that'll work," I said. "Let's try it."

So we did. We were taking a chance, going another way to the restaurant. But maybe, just maybe we would be able to –

Coming to the corner, Laura staggered to a halt.

"Uh, guys?" she said. "We've got trouble."

Icy fear shot through my veins as I saw that the alley up ahead was blocked...

By even more vampires.

17

"What do we do? What do we do?" Laura asked.

"Someone call Lockwood," I said, keeping my eyes glued on the vamps up ahead. They weren't charging. Yet. They were all geared up, ready to fight, fingers twitching at their sides. But they weren't charging.

I could feel each beat of my heart, each pulse of the blood moving through my veins. Could they smell it? Was the fear mingling with the smell of my blood, driving them crazy?

"No signal," Xandra said. "I don't know, cell towers must be busy."

"Everyone is calling 911 right now," Derrick said. He grit his teeth, his hands balling into fists.

Of course they were. It couldn't be easy, could it?

Mill and Iona appeared around the corner, bringing up the rear of our little caravan. "Are you freaking kidding me?" Iona asked. She had a long, black gash across her neck down to her collarbone. I guess these vampires meant business.

"We can't go back." Mill's shirt was torn at the shoulder, and his knee was visible through a rip in his pants; both places were black with his own ebon blood. "They're right behind us."

"Well, we can't go forward," Xandra said.

"Why aren't they attacking?" Laura asked. "It doesn't make any sense."

"They're funneling us," Mill said. "Trying to direct us somewhere."

"Where?" Gregory asked.

"How should I know?" Mill spat, glaring at Gregory.

"Well, then we need to go somewhere else," I said, racking my brain for options.

"Yeah, but where?" Xandra asked.

I glanced into the busy road beside us, traffic streaming by. This was stupid. I knew it was. Before the words even escaped my mouth, I knew that I was going to sound like a complete lunatic.

If I wasn't terrified out of my wits, then I would have probably been a little more rational about it. But in the situation, yeah, rationality was out the window.

"We go sideways," I said. "Into traffic."

"Are you out of your mind?" Laura asked. "That's suicide." A car shot by at forty miles an hour, illustrating her point.

"It's either that, or we get eaten by vamps. Your choice," I said.

She frowned. Xandra looked at me like I had grown three heads.

"This is not a good idea – " Iona started.

But I had built up just enough courage to run.

I pelted out onto the street, hearing the pounding footsteps of the others behind me and beside me as they followed after me. Horns honked and lights flared as cars came hurtling toward us. I heard Xandra let out a shriek as a car came and missed her by inches, tires squealing as they came to a swift halt.

The vampires that followed after us didn't seem to care about the cars. They leapt onto their roofs, diving back onto the street with their predatory grace. There was a squeal of tires, and a vampire got struck right in the side. The car screeched to halt, but the vampire was already up and running again, shaking it off. Another got clipped by a side mirror, and the shattering of glass joined the noisy chorus on the street.

I looked all around me as I ran around the back of a stopped car, trying to account for all my friends. Xandra was right behind me. Derrick, not far ahead. Gregory – where was Gregory?

I caught a glimpse of him sliding across the hood of a car that was idling far too close to the car in front of it. He landed on the other side and kept running.

A shout drew my attention from him and I staggered to a stop. Laura was a few cars down, and a vampire had caught onto the back of her hair, holding her in place.

My heart hammered against my chest. No, no, no – this couldn't–

I started toward her, and saw Iona change directions at the same time. She had seen it, too. More horns blared, headlamps flashed. But we didn't need to it seemed, because Laura brandished her stake and turned, shoving it into the wrist of the vampire who was holding her in place. The vampire shrieked in pain, and dropped her. Laura took off as soon as the vampire's grip loosened.

"Are you okay?" I called.

"Fine," she called back.

But I wasn't exactly fine. I heard a snicker and realized that I had stopped for half a second too long.

Another vampire had caught up with me. Tall, gangly, with a dozen or so piercings in his ears and lip, he was sneering at me as he hurtled over the top of a soft top convertible as if it were no higher than a stair.

But I was ready. Before he landed, I lashed out with my foot, sending him to the ground. A sharp kick that I had been practicing with Mill for ages, it sent a shockwave through my body, and I could have sworn that I tore a muscle in my leg doing it. But I did it. And it had worked. I couldn't believe it worked.

The thrill of success flushed through me, giving me a renewed strength. The traffic had just picked up again, and the car that I was standing in front of honked its horn at me. I turned to yell at the car; *Did you not just see what happened?*

But the lane where the vampire had fallen was empty, and I watched him get back to his feet, his teeth bared at me–

And then a black Hummer came whizzing by, running over the vampire without even stopping.

I stood there for a second, staring at the mangled body of the vampire on the ground, black blood smearing the ground. Then I took off toward the sidewalk, which was just a few paces ahead of me. "Is everyone okay?"

None of us were runners, and none of us were equipped for a long sprint like this. I mentally checked roll as I looked; we were all here. All except Mill and Iona.

I looked back out into the traffic. We'd managed to stop several lanes, and caused more than one fender bender. People were standing outside of their cars, yelling at one another, car horns were blaring furiously. No one seemed to notice the vampires leaping around and above the cars straight toward us. But they were still pursuing, despite the chaos going on around us.

"Is that – is that the place?"

I looked up the street where Derrick was pointing, and my heart leapt. The brightly lit sign of Pan e Vino shone up ahead like a beacon in the darkest night.

"That's it!" I shouted. "Let's go!"

We could still make it. We could get out of this alive.

And then...

Well.

We would deal with what came next when we got there.

18

"This might have been...very pleasant...if we weren't running for our lives," Xandra said between pants.

Night had fallen in earnest, the hazy light pollution of the city hanging in the sky to the south. There were people all around us who were having perfectly normal nights, not being chased by vampires. And that seemed like an impossibility to me in that moment.

"How many are still following us?" Derrick asked.

"Hard to say," Mill said, appearing out of nowhere. "But for every one we manage to take out, another appears."

"They aren't fighters, most of them," Iona said, appearing suddenly at my other side. "But Mill was right. They're definitely trying to herd us somewhere."

"Like the cattle we are, huh?" I asked dryly.

The restaurant was only two blocks away and I had never wanted to get to a place more in my entire life. The longing was so sharp, so clear, that if I would just reach out, I felt like I'd be able to grab it firmly with both of my hands.

But we were all worn out. Exhausted. I could hear everyone panting, their faces covered in glistening sweat, their best clothes ruined by the attacks and the running. Our pace was flagging, and every meter we covered it slowed further.

A screaming siren rent the air as we reached another street to cross, and the flashing red and white lights of an ambulance danced on the surface of the buildings on either side of the street. Two firetrucks followed in close pursuit. Cars strained to get out of the way as the ambulance honked its horn, causing all of us to cover our ears from the sharp sound.

"Oh, crap," Derrick yelled.

We couldn't cross, not when the cars were all crammed together, trying to get out of the way of the emergency services vehicles.

This was not good.

I turned around to see Mill and Iona standing behind us like guards, their arms outstretched in defensive positions. We only had to wait another few seconds at most, and then we could just run across the street like we did before–

But those seconds were seemingly endless.

Had the ambulance stopped? Why hadn't the traffic started moving again?

"Move it!" I cried out into the street. "Get out of the way!"

The cars were nearly hopping the curb as they tried to get back on the road, the ambulance still blaring its horn. The nearest vampires pursuing us threw themselves at Iona and Mill, not holding back their immense strength as they did. It sounded terrible when they crashed into each other, their limbs thudding against their steel-like flesh. I'd experienced that for myself, fighting vampires, how hearty they were, how hard they hit. Watching them fight one another was a terrible thing to behold.

"They must be going to help the people outside the

theater," Laura said, staring after the ambulance as it headed down the street. "I hope they get there in time." The image of the people on the ground flashed across my mind, but I pushed it aside. I didn't have time to deal with that kind of horror right now, not when another was staring me in the face.

Three vampires jumped on Mill all at once, and another tried to bolt past him to get to us. In amazement, we watched as Mill reached out to the one who had gotten past him and yanked him back, all while the other three were ganging up on him. Claw-like fingernails flashed, and black blood flew everywhere.

Iona hurled away the vampire that had attacked her, and grabbed one off of Mill, plunging a stake right through his back into his heart. He jerked and spasmed, then started to dissolve into black goo.

"This is insane," said Gregory. The disbelief in his voice reflected all of our thoughts. "They just keep coming. I've seen this movie. And it doesn't end well."

He was right. I watched in horror as more poured down the sidewalk toward us, like a swarm of angry hornets.

"Cars are moving again," Xandra said. "We should go."

"I still can't get ahold of Lockwood," Derrick said as we started to run again, pressing his phone to his ear. "It just won't connect."

"Don't worry," I said. "As soon as he sees us running, he'll help us to get out of here as quickly as he can."

I had to keep telling myself that. Lockwood would know we were there. His super faerie hearing would detect us coming, over the sirens and the screams and all the other street chaos.

The restaurant was there, right there, only a few buildings away. We were so close.

"Cassie!"

I wheeled around and found the face of a vampire right in mine. His face covered in blood, he dove at me.

Another car slammed on its brakes right in front of us, tires screeching, causing us to jump out of the way.

It seemed that the vampire and I were on the same brainwave, though, because we both took the opportunity to strike at the other. He lashed out with his hands, going for my neck. I, on the other hand, ducked before shoving my hand upward into his chest, sinking the stake into his hard, stony flesh. He cried out and leapt away, holding the hole I had made just beside his shoulder.

I gritted my teeth. Missed the heart. I was losing my touch.

He went to dive at me again, but Xandra was there, her stake high in the air, and she plunged it right between his shoulder blades. He jerked one last time, and Xandra shoved his limp body to the side as he began to dissolve, nodding at me, her hair all mussed from the run. "You all right?"

"Thanks to you," I said.

"Cassie, Mill is hurt," I heard from behind her. Laura was pointing back at the sidewalk, and I could see Iona trying to help Mill to his feet. The vampires they had been fighting were in pain, on the ground, but the pair of them didn't seem to be much better.

"I don't understand," I said, the fear threatening to take over. Mill was hurt, and I felt like I was hurting, too. I stumbled my way toward him, but Iona waved her hand at me, telling me to back off.

My legs were frozen all of the sudden. My mind was racing and foggy. Horns were honking, people yelling out of their car windows for me to move, others screaming wondering why there were bodies in the street and on the sidewalk.

But I couldn't get my brain to function.

"Cassie, we need to run," came Xandra's voice.

I felt someone's hand close around my wrist and yank me away, off the street and up onto the sidewalk on the other side. "We're almost there," Laura said, firmly. She had me by the wrist and was pulling me to the finish line. A look back showed that Iona had Mill, and she was dragging him with us. Black blood slicked the front of his shirt, and took my breath away.

I knew that I shouldn't have trusted Lord Varycas. It was all too good to be true. He lulled me into a false sense of security and then *wham*. Came at me when I least expected it.

"Come on, we can make it," Derrick said.

Our bare feet slapped against the concrete, nearly covered over by our frantic breathing. The vampires snarled behind us, pursuing, making my heart want to burst out of my chest in fear and uncertainty.

Would we make it?

And if we did...would Mill be all right?

I slammed into someone's back as they came to a stop just a dozen yards from the restaurant. It was Gregory, and he was staring at something in front of him.

"What is i– "

But the words faltered on my tongue as I peered over his shoulder...

And saw Jacquelyn and Lord Varycas's chief enforcer, Jo, standing just in front of the restaurant...

Waiting for us.

19

I t was Jacquelyn. It was Jacquelyn all along.
    Not Varycas.

Oh, how could I have been so stupid? She had been at the meeting with him, hadn't said a word the entire time. Just glared at me with those hateful eyes, wishing that I would just drop dead on the spot. And now here she was, grinning at me with her evil, pale face, snickering as she did.

"Going somewhere?" Jacquelyn asked, tossing her braid over her shoulder, her arms folded over her chest casually, as if we had just bumped into each other at the mall, and she was ready to bully me like a middle schooler. Jo was hovering just behind her, easily twice Jacquelyn's size in height and width. She was glaring at me as if I had done some sort of terrible wrong to her.

Iona and Mill caught up to us. Mill hung back, barely upright, but keeping his body between the others and the vampires still pursuing us. Blood covered Iona's whole left arm, and I couldn't tell if it was hers or someone else's. Still, she moved up to stand beside me.

"Jacquelyn, there are innocent people here," I said.

"Oh, no," Jacquelyn said, putting her hands to her cheeks, mock-frightened. "We might spook the cattle." Then she cackled.

"You want to fight me? Fine," I said. "Fight me. And we can settle this like adults." Brave talk considering the vamps on my side looked like they'd been in a war. Meanwhile, Jacquelyn was fresh as a daisy, and backed up by a hulking beast and a small army. Still, I clenched my stake in hand, felt my sweaty palm slip against the wood.

Jacquelyn laughed out loud. "Like adults? Funny story: I'll never be an adult, because you brought a bunch of vampires to our hometown and robbed me of the chance. So...I can't settle anything like an adult."

"I never intended for any of this to–"

"I don't want some halfhearted apology," she said. "Begging? That I could maybe stand to listen to for an hour or so before you die. And screaming. Yes. Definitely want some serious screaming. But you can keep your apologies."

My mind was racing. Where was Lockwood? Had Jacquelyn and Jo gotten to him? Or was he waiting, oblivious, down a side street? If we could get the limo over here, at least some of them might be able to escape.

I had to stall. But I also had to know.

"What about the peace talks?" I asked. "Were they all lies?"

"You'd know all about lies, wouldn't you?" She leered, arching an eyebrow at me. "Still...I'm a big girl now." She smirked. "I make my own decisions. There have been too many things in my life where someone has made the choice for me. I'm done with that."

She was being a little drama queen, wasn't she? I glared at her. "Fine. You want to make this between you and me? Let everyone else go, and we can hash it out. Sound good?"

Jacquelyn laughed, a cackle that grated on my ears.

"You're funny. You'd just love a chance to play the noble hero again, wouldn't you? A liar and a martyr, I bet you'd get off on that. But it's not gonna happen." Danger flashed in her eyes. "No, it hurts you when your friends get hurt." Jacquelyn snapped her fingers, and a wicked grin spread over her face.

"Jacquelyn, don't do this," I said. I could hear the tremble in my words, but this didn't exactly seem like the time to let my pride get in the way. "What exactly do you want?"

Jacquelyn's eyes narrowed as she stared at me. "What do I want? I want my life back, you idiot. I want everything that you stole from me. I hate your guts. I want you dead."

I knew that was what she wanted, ultimately, but to actually hear her say it hurt me more than I thought it would. My heart broke all over again as I stared into the face of the girl who was once one of my very best friends. Guilt racked me, piercing all the way down to my bones.

"I'm...sorry," I said.

"Ugh," Jacquelyn said. "Whatever." As though the very taste of emotion and sentiment appalled her. She motioned with her hand, and the vampires that had been following started to close in again.

"You're going to regret this." Iona's words came out strong, harsh, even guttural, completely at odds with the way she looked right now. Except for the blood.

"I doubt it," Jacquelyn said. "In case you missed it, I sort of have all of the control right now."

"Not if I snap your neck and stake you right here and now," Iona said. "Before you manage to carry out your master plan."

A cold shock ran through me. "Iona, don't– "

Jacquelyn looked over at Jo. "Take out her vamp friends. I can't have them in the way."

Jo lashed out at Iona, faster than I would have believed possible, even from a vampire.

"No!" I shouted.

But Jo had already struck Iona, who staggered back. Anguish gripped Iona's face as fresh, dark blood gushed out of a wound in her upper arm, glistening in the light of the streetlamps.

20

T his couldn't be happening. I was so helpless. I couldn't do anything. I was at the mercy of these stupid vampires, and there was nothing that I could do about it. Iona sputtered and gurgled, her legs flailing, her fingers grasping at the gushing wound.

My chest heaved as I stared up at her, too horrified to look away.

Iona crumpled to a knee. Dark blood started to spread across the sidewalk like a pool of oil. She tried to lift her arm, but it didn't move. I rushed to her, kneeling beside her. My knees were like jelly, and there was a burning in my chest, making it hard for me to breathe. Her gaze was flicking in and out of focus as she stared up at my face.

"Iona, stay with me," I said. My eyes stung with tears. This wasn't happening. It couldn't be. "Everything is going to be fine."

Was I saying that to help her to feel better? Or was it so I could keep on going?

"Another lie," Jacquelyn said with amused triumph. "Big surprise."

Iona gritted her teeth together, blood highlighting the white between them. "Cassie...duck."

I cocked my head at her; I was already on one knee. I looked up, saw Jo looming over us, just an arm's length away, leering, and wondered why Iona would have said that–

There was a flash of green light, and Jo was knocked off her feet.

"Lockwood!" Laura cried out.

My head snapped up.

Sure enough, there was Lockwood, wearing his best navy blue suit. He stood just out of sight of the windows at the restaurant, another ball of green light forming in his hands. And he looked pissed, the glow making his cheek-bones prominent, and his eyes glint with rage.

"Get away from them," he said, pointing the light at Jacquelyn.

Hope flooded through me, making me light headed. We weren't alone, after all.

Jacquelyn's eyes widened, but her smirk remained in place. "One of the faerie? Where'd you come from?"

"From the land of Faerie, of course," he said, taking a few slow steps forward. "A more important question – where do you think you'll go after I kill you? I'm not well versed with vampire theology, if any, and it's a point of curiosity for me." The green glow throbbed, and gave his eyes a malicious look utterly unlike the Lockwood I knew.

I wanted to call out to him, to thank him for coming. But the words were lost in my mind as Iona let out a gurgle of pain, her back arching.

Jacquelyn looked down at Jo, who was struggling to her feet, her pink mohawk askew. "Get up, you worthless piece of–"

"Don't you tell me what to do," Jo said. She spat, and black blood flecked the ground at her feet.

"We have to get to the limo," Xandra said softly from behind me, wielding her stake.

"Someone help me carry Iona," I said, my voice trembling. I couldn't believe that she had collapsed like she had.

"I'll help you," Derrick said, coming over to us. Vampires were hissing around us, moving in for the kill like circling sharks. But there were too many sounds, too many colors and lights. Too much going on. My head was pounding, and I felt completely drained.

Lockwood was suddenly in the air over us, vaulting over us as if we were nothing. He landed deftly on the sidewalk beside Mill, who was struggling. He shoved aside a vampire, sending the guy sprawling into traffic, but the sheer volume of black blood coating him made him look like he'd just climbed out of a tar pit.

And just how many vampires were there? I thought I had killed them all in Draven's condo. Where had Jacquelyn found these flunkies?

A stir of motion behind her drew my attention. Jacquelyn leered at me, because she saw it, too–

There were a host of diners coming out of the restaurant. A family; wife, husband, three kids, one cradled in mom's arms with a blue onesie wrapped around him. He had fat little thighs and chubby little cheeks and he was the only one looking our way as a Jacquelyn gestured with her hand and half a dozen vamps broke off, heading right for them.

I stared, horrorstruck. Jacquelyn watched me as they blurred through the warm evening toward their helpless victims.

"Remember that deal you cut to save your own skin?" Jacquelyn asked, grinning. "How you'd sit back and say nothing, do nothing, while we did our thing?" She licked her lips. "Bet you didn't think you'd have to watch it happen."

I couldn't even help myself; I leapt forward and Jo speared me in the back of the head with a hard punch that I didn't see coming. I slammed into the sidewalk, my lights going out for a moment. When I raised my head again–

The vamps were all over that family.

"No!" I shouted, and slammed into Jo's leg just below the knee. I must have caught her by surprise, because she staggered even though her leg felt like I'd chop blocked a tree trunk. My arm and shoulder hurt like hell, and my bare feet skidded violently against the rough concrete sidewalk, tearing skin. I hurried forward, brandishing my stake in hand.

I couldn't let this happen. A vampire had the mother, screaming, by her hair, and was pulling her head back, ready to sink his teeth into her neck.

Something caught me; the hem of my dress, and I heard it rip, but I didn't care. I charged forward as the vampire brought his teeth down...

I stopped, my body jerking violently against the limits of my dress. I turned my head to see Jacquelyn there; she'd seized me by the body of the garment now, and there was no getting away from her without fully ripping it apart. "You're working harder to save strangers than you did to save me," she said, a hint of bitterness making its way out as she spoke through her teeth.

"They're innocent," I said, and thrust my arm out to full extension, plunging the stake into the vamp's back just as he prepared to feed. He jerked violently and dropped the woman, who screamed and ripped loose of his falling body.

She ran, baby in hand, into one of the vampires holding another of her children, knocking him over.

Jacquelyn tore hard at my dress, bringing me around in a snarl so that I couldn't see any longer. "So was I." She slapped me across the face and it felt like running into a brick wall. I spun and hit the ground, stunned at the pain flaring across my cheek. Darkness threatened to drag me into its depths, my head swimming from the strength of the blow and the tiredness of the night's events.

"It sucks, doesn't it?" Jacquelyn said. She sounded about a million miles away. "Watching things like this unfold around you, and knowing that you're so helpless to do anything to change it?"

I turned to look at her. Beyond her, I could see Mill struggling, futilely, against a vampire in a leather biker jacket. Lockwood was throwing green spell magic at a vamp wearing a big, red ribbon in her hair. Jo had Iona in a death grip and was squeezing her violently. Iona, always pale, looked somehow even more pasty.

And Jacquelyn just stood over me, radiating spite. I suddenly regretted every moment I had ever spent with her. Every laugh we had shared, every phone call, every study date. It didn't matter that we had spent half our childhoods sleeping over at each other's houses, staying up half the night laughing and talking. It didn't matter that we had swapped perfume-scented, neon-inked notes in class, gossiping about the boys we liked. And it didn't matter that what I did to her...what happened before I moved to Florida was my biggest regret.

I had never hated another person so much. I hadn't even known it was possible until this moment.

In her eyes, I saw a similar fire that would never cool. She hated me just as much as I now hated her, and she had ever since she'd been reborn a vampire. I'd hoped, some-where deep within me, that she and I could be like Iona and I were, or Mill and I were (minus the kissy kissy).

Looking in her eyes now...I knew that it would never happen.

She hated me with a fire that would burn, always.

And there was nothing left for me to do but hate her right back.

21

A t what point does someone give up, and admit to themselves that they are about to die? I mean, it has to be a decision, right? A moment when you stop fighting? When you realize that everything is completely out of your control, and you are at the mercy of the circumstances around you?

Sickness, car accidents, old age...or vampires attacking right out in the open, taking down civilians right in front of me.

"Cassie!"

I heard my name, but it was like someone had turned something off in my brain. I tried to stand, tried to move, but Jacquelyn still had me snugly by the dress. She hauled me to my feet, but when I tried to move, she cackled, yanking me back. I spun in a short circle, seeing–

I could see Lockwood tossing balls of green light at vampires, hitting them square in the chest. I could smell the acrid stench of vampire blood mingling with the metallic tang of human blood. I could hear the screams of terror, the laughter of the vampires, and the thud as their strikes made contact with those I cared about.

"Cassie!"

"They're calling your name," Jacquelyn whispered, pulling me close to her. She snugged a steely arm around my neck, then rocked me back and forth like a baby. "Do you hear them? Begging you to save them. As if you could," she laughed.

Her laughter was acid poured in my ears. The fire I'd felt awakening in my heart moments before, when I started to truly hate my old friend, and everything she represented, stirred from the embers of my weariness.

Through the fog of tiredness, I saw Laura and Derrick trying to hoist Iona up onto her feet. She was conscious, cringing in pain, black blood running down her chin.

Some of the fog lifted, but the fear and anger took its place.

"She can't walk on her own," Laura said, sounding very far away. "We need to get her away from here." Vampires swarmed behind them, closing.

"Do you know what it feels like to die?" Jacquelyn asked. "I do. Wouldn't recommend it." She laughed again. "Say...when your friends die, do you think they'll come back hating you as much as I do?"

My heart didn't feel like it could take much more. I wished in that moment she'd just plunge her teeth into my neck and get it over with. She turned me around, and I saw Mill on his knees, grasping as his side. Blood was dripping between his fingers. He looked up at me said, "I can't...can't go any further." And he sagged to all fours.

He couldn't get to his feet. The vampires loomed all around, ready to descend.

My heart was racing, making me light headed. Jacquelyn's arm was anchored to my neck.

"The thing about dying to a vampire," Jacquelyn said, "is that you fight and fight, and it doesn't do any good. They're just...too strong. It's like going up against the tide. It will eventually knock you down, and it'll never even notice the inconvenience of you. That's your problem, Cassie." She laughed. "You picked a fight with the very forces of nature. Things you can't comprehend with that tiny brain of yours."

I wobbled on unsteady feet, my vision swimming. "You know what? You're right," I said. "I never really had a chance."

Jacquelyn stiffened against me. "No...you didn't."

"Jacquelyn?" I held myself up, lightly, against her arm.

"Yes?"

"I lied." With the stake in my hand – which she'd either forgotten about, or just did not give a fig that I had – I rammed it down and into Jacquelyn's thigh, prompted her to scream an unearthly vampire scream and immediately drop me to deal with more urgent matters. Like the iron tip and splinters I'd just jammed three inches into her leg.

I sprawled when she cut me loose, nearly eating concrete and dinging my knee as I hit the ground. Another vampire appeared, coming straight at me now that Jacquelyn had let go of me. He charged, arms wide, teeth exposed, leading with his chest.

I didn't even think about it. I brought my stake up square into the vampire's chest.

It collapsed onto the ground, becoming a pile of black goo as it did.

Another vampire came at me from the left, blurring swiftly into view, but my instincts took over. I plunged the same stake right into its chest, and it too crumpled to the ground.

Three more came, and my mind was completely blank as I engaged with them, my body falling into the muscle memory taught to me by Mill. Trip them up, duck underneath their blows. I even took a scratch to the face, but couldn't care at all about it. I let that bloodlust that I had shoved aside for so long come out to play, and it was vicious.

I was not helpless. I was not some fragile little flower that they could smash beneath their boots. I was not going to let them get away with this. They wanted a fight? They were going to get a fight.

Cassie the Slayer had been reborn.

"Cassie, look out – "

But I was ready. The vampire that I had kicked beneath the tires of the Hummer was there, swinging at me with his fingernails the way a werewolf would. I took a slice to the shoulder, but I felt no pain as I drove my stake up underneath his jaw.

His eyes rolled into the back of his head, gurgling from the hole in his throat. I yanked the stake out, and drove it into his chest where his dead heart lay. He cried out in pain, collapsing to the ground at my feet, features already beginning to dissolve.

Another vampire stepped in front of me, her teeth bared, her lip curling.

I was exhausted. My limbs ached and wobbled. My hand trembled that held my stake. The stitch in my side had grown even worse.

A ball of green light shot past me, hitting the vamp square in the chest. She flew back into traffic and a car slammed into her, sending her spiraling across the street.

Lockwood appeared beside me. He had new scratches

on his cheek, silvery blood shining in the light of the street-lamps. "Get the others," he said. "And get to the limo. Go."

"How are we going to–"

"Go," he spat. And then he erected another forcefield like he had created at Byron's house when the witches attacked us. "I won't be able to hold this for more than a minute or so. Now go!"

I stared at him dully for a second, then waved Derrick and Laura on. They were staggering under Iona's weight a distance ahead of me. Xandra hurried after, as did Gregory. I tried to not notice the way Gregory was limping. "Where's Mill?" I called.

"Just go," Lockwood said. "I'll bring him. Hurry!"

I hesitated for a half a second more before realizing I was putting everyone else in danger by waiting.

Jacquelyn was trapped behind the barrier that Lockwood had made, and she pounded against it with her fists, blood streaming down her knuckles. We stared at each other for a moment. I could see Jo on the ground, a burned hole from where one of Lockwood's spells had struck her.

I started to run after the others, pelting barefoot across the rough pavement toward the parking lot at the back of the restaurant. My feet were bleeding, but I couldn't take time to redress even those most nagging and least of wounds. As we passed the restaurant, I saw a body splayed out on the sidewalk, bleeding from the neck.

It was the father from that family that had walked out the door minutes before. Wrong place, wrong time. Hopefully the wife and kids got away. I knew by the unmoving nature of his eyes that he was dead. Not so much a twitch.

I staggered, unable to look away. Like driving past a horrific car accident, seeing the tarp covering the road with a shape of a person beneath it. Wicked, morbid curiosity kept my eyes glued to their horrorstruck faces.

He was dead because of me, but I had zero time to contemplate that right now. I had to keep moving. I couldn't stop. I needed to escape with the others. They were my priority now. I hurried toward the corner ahead, beyond which I could see the parking lot. My friends had already rounded it, and I was determined not to slow. I needed to keep up, to escape with them, so that Lockwood's sacrifice – if he was making one, right now – would not be in vain.

I was light headed as I came around the corner toward the parking lot when I froze.

"Hey," I shouted, readying my stake once more. A vampire bathed in the shadow of the restaurant building was hunched over a body of a human dressed in a fine black suit, with polished black shoes. He was eerily still, his hands splayed out at his sides, limply facing toward the sky. I didn't recognize him, but I saw from him the same dead eyes as the father around the corner had. Another innocent victim. The vampire was leaning over, his teeth pressed into the corpse's neck–

"Get away from him you, monster–" I said, unable to muster the strength to just walk up and stab him in the back. I was so tired, my legs felt like dead things that barely supported my weight. The adrenaline had clearly subsided, and I was in the process of coming down from my high. I kept my stake positioned over my chest, in case he decided to bum rush me, he'd impale himself.

He didn't, though. The vampire turned his face up toward me...and my whole world flipped upside down.

It was Mill.

Mill.

Mill was feeding on an innocent human.

His lips, lips that I had kissed countless times now, were shining with blood. It dripped down his chin in perfect, round beads. It was dark red against his pale, stony skin. It had run down his neck in a spiderweb pattern and onto the pristine white shirt that he had picked out specifically to wear to the theater tonight. It spread like blots of ink on paper across his collar, streaked across his chest like watercolor paint on a canvas.

But it wasn't ink. It wasn't paint. It was blood. Human blood. Blood that had just left the veins of a living, breathing person. An innocent person.

The skin of the human's hand was so pale now...so papery looking. So...wrinkled.

I just stared at him. Fear like I had never known gripped my heart. Betrayal so profound that I was having trouble staying upright. In all of my nightmares in the past few months, the vampires that I saw in dream after dream had never been Mill. Not once. I never imagined that he could – that he would–

The metallic stench of the blood hit me, and I recoiled.

"Cassie..." he said, letting the body fall to the ground, getting up to come closer to me. His teeth were pointed, dripping with crimson.

I threw up my hands to block him from coming any closer. "No..." I said. "I – I don't – "

Words were lost to me.

Mill was a vampire...but in my heart, I hadn't ever really believed it until that exact moment.

22

Time stopped, I was pretty sure. The other vampires didn't matter. Lockwood's command didn't matter. Getting to the limo didn't matter.

I couldn't wrap my mind around it. Mill, who was always so conscious of his humanity, who did everything in his power to help me preserve my own, had none on display now. In all the time I'd known him, he had never once been overcome with the desire to feed like this. I knew he needed blood, but I also knew that he kept his fridge fully stocked, just like Iona did. He was not the sort to simply feed on some stranger in an alley.

Or so I thought.

Until now, I had been able to separate Mill and Iona in my mind from the other vampires that I had seen. They weren't like the others. They had showed me time and time again that they were more human than not.

But now...

Everything that I believed had been ripped to shreds right in front of me.

Mill was just as much of a monster as Byron was.

And that was more than I could take.

He hastily wiped his face off on the sleeve of his jacket, the human's blood streaking the cloth. "We need to go," he said, reaching out to me with a bloody hand.

I jerked away, recoiling from his scarlet-dripping visage.

"Cassie!" Xandra shouted. She was at the edge of the parking lot, off to my right. Under the bright lights, I could see Laura and Derrick struggling with Iona across the pavement. The limo was there, parked within sight.

We were so close.

I heard Mill say my name, but I ignored him and took off toward the parking lot, bile rising in my throat. I headed for the limo, and when I got close, Xandra was waiting. "What's wrong?" she asked.

"Nothing," I said automatically. A lie. And I didn't even care in that moment. It wasn't important right now.

Not important? Yeah right, it was probably one of the most important things to me. I had just seen humans die because my psychotic ex-best friend just sent vampires after my friends and me. Every one of us had been injured, and Lockwood was still in the thick of it. My boyfriend...probably just ended the life of a person.

My boyfriend...was a monster.

I ran past her toward the limo. Mill caught up with me, and was staring hard at the side of my face. I ignored him, unable to make eye contact. I didn't know what to say, and now didn't seem like the time to have a full-blown explosive sort of argument about how wrong it is to kill people in plain sight of your human girlfriend.

He was back to his full strength, I realized as he tore past me to get to the limo. My stomach twisted into painful knots as I realized the reason why.

"Let's get her in first," Derrick said, struggling under the weight of Iona, who was limp as any of the dead. The parking lot was quiet, almost filled with cars. Laura yanked on the door of the limo, and with a sigh of relief, found it open.

"Gentle, gentle," she said as she and Derrick tried to ease Iona inside. They were careful to not crack her head as they lowered her in.

"How are we getting out of here?" I said, a new fear washing over me. We would be sitting ducks in a limo like this that wasn't moving. "Lockwood didn't give me–"

Gregory waved a key in front of my face as he headed for the driver's side door. "I got it. Let's move."

"Is everyone here?" I asked, sliding into the back behind Derrick.

Mill slid in after me. I moved up to the seat behind the divider.

"Everyone except Lockwood," Gregory said. "And he said he would catch up."

I almost launched into an argument with him about why we needed to stay, but I knew that Lockwood would likely kill me himself if he knew that I was stalling for him.

I looked over at Iona, who Laura had spread out across one of the side seats. As a vampire, I couldn't exactly check for a pulse or the rise and fall of her chest to see if she was alive or not. No, I had to rely on the fact that since she was a vampire, she would probably just need to rest for a while.

"She's going to be okay, right?" I asked from the seat opposite Laura.

"She'll be fine," Mill said roughly. "But she needs blood."

"So she is still alive?" I asked, still staring intently at Iona's face. I couldn't bring myself to look over at him, knowing the evidence of red that covered his collar and his front.

"As alive as any vampire can be," he said. There was a heaviness in his words, but I couldn't be sure it was just wishful thinking on my part. He could have chosen not to feed on that man.

"She's not conscious," Laura said, dabbing at one of Iona's wounds. There seemed to be...so many. "She was a few minutes ago. I – I don't know what happened."

"How in the world do you start this thing?" Gregory said from up in the front.

"We better get moving," Xandra said. "Or we're going to get swarmed."

"I am aware of that," Gregory snapped. "But I can't find the ignition – "

"You idiot," Xandra said, climbing into the seat behind him. She stared through the open divider, pointing with her finger. "It's a button start. See that big blue circle there on the dash?"

The engine roared to life as Gregory made a whoop of success.

"Now hit the gas," Xandra said. "And get us the hell out of here."

23

"Um, guys? How am I supposed to reverse this?" Gregory shouted once the engine was purring. The car smelled like blood and...well, vampire blood. Which smelled much worse than the metallic scent of the human variety.

"Just go!" Xandra said. She was sitting right beside me just behind the divider.

It had to be something, didn't it? None of this could ever be easy. Even trying to escape.

Gregory turned around and shot her a dirty look. "Um, do you not see the long line of cars beside me?"

"And you're worried about...what? Dinging the paint? We're being attacked by vampires, scrape the damned side and get us out here!" Xandra shouted.

"We don't have much time," I said. "Lockwood said we would only have a minute or so of a head start."

Gregory rolled his shoulders and gripped onto the steering wheel with both hands. "Well, here goes nothing." And he promptly backed up, going from zero to twenty with a hard jerk of the transmission, and a grinding scrape as he ripped the limo's bumper across the (once) spotless finish of a vintage Porsche.

"Attaboy," Xandra said, clapping him on the back. "Just think of it as stimulating the body shop industry in Tampa."

I cringed. Lockwood was going to kill me for letting him drive.

"I feel like I just committed a war crime," Gregory said, throwing the limo into drive and flooring it. He bumped forward and into the back of a Lexus SUV, jarring us all.

"Now finish your three-point turn without making it a five point turn and let's get outta here!" Xandra said. There were bright spots of color in her cheeks, and the dress she was wearing was torn across the abdomen. Aside from some shallow cuts along her arms and knees, she was in pretty good shape. Thank God that she'd learned to take care of herself after hanging out with me for all these months.

"You know," Gregory said, hitting the gas, "I only got my license six months ago, and the only thing I've driven was my mom's Kia."

"Great, so you should be used to driving without fear of causing any damage to your vehicle," Xandra said. "Now step on it, learner's permit."

"Easy, will you? We've got wounded back here," Laura snapped. She was sitting against the back seat with Iona, still dabbing at the wounds. She nearly fell off as Gregory ran over the curb bringing us onto the street.

"Sorry, Iona," Gregory said, peering through the rearview mirror. "Oh, God–"

He swerved the steering wheel, jerking it hard to the right.

All of us were pitched to the side, slamming into the windows and one another. My shoulder collided with the plastic handle of the door, sending sharp pains up my side.

Guess I was in worse shape than I thought; was I wounded on that arm, too?

"What was that?" Xandra said, brushing her blue hair from her eyes as she sat up, gripping the inside of the divider, glaring at Gregory with a fire in her eyes.

"Sorry, I just thought I was gonna hit someone – oh, crap."

Another hard yank of the wheel, but at least this time we were prepared for it.

"Are you sure you actually passed your driver's test?" Laura called.

"Ha, ha, very funny," Gregory said, wiping his forehead with the back of his hand. He put his foot down on the gas and we started speeding down an empty side street.

I looked around and saw Derrick sitting with his hands crossed in his lap, staring down at the floor. Kinda weird in the midst of all this. "Hey, are you okay?" I asked. He didn't reply. "Derrick?" I asked again.

"Maybe he needs a minute," Mill said.

I ignored Mill and moved over to sit beside Derrick.

There was a haunted look in his eyes, a deep-seated anger that was burning, raging at something inside his mind. "Hey…" I said, even more gently.

Mill made a sound of frustration, but again, I ignored him.

Derrick looked up at me, his blue eyes piercing. There was a long scratch just under his eye, and the skin below his left ear was coated in the tacky, tar-like blood of the vampires. "I was…totally unprepared," he said quietly. "I just…I had no idea what to do."

"Hey, that makes all of us," I said, trying to be as encouraging as possible.

Gregory let out a scream from the front, making me

wheel around, my heart starting to race. But he had just activated the wind shield wipers, which were beating against the window hard and fast, making a small squeak as they scraped across the dry surface.

"It's cool, it's cool," Gregory said. "I got this–" He fumbled about the wheel, but all he managed to do was turn on the limo's brights. "Oh, crap."

I looked back at Derrick. "Seriously, don't beat yourself up. We all got away. And you were a huge help out there."

Derrick didn't say anything. The muscles in his jaw tightened, and he looked back down at the floor. He had lost all of the wind from his sails. I didn't have time to play counselor, though. I had my own problems to deal with.

There was a loud *bang* against the top of the limo, and we all screamed as one. How had they managed to catch up with us so fast? If Gregory had gotten the limo out of the parking lot faster –

There was a rap on the sunroof, followed by a muffled voice. "Kindly let me in."

"Lockwood!" I crawled over to the seat beside Xandra and leaned over to Gregory. "Open the sunroof."

"Bro, I can't even turn the high beams off. You want me to find the sunroof button? Good luck."

Xandra's eyes narrowed as she thrust her upper body into the driver's compartment, reached up to the roof, and mashed a button near the interior lights. There was a hum from behind us, and a *shlump* as Lockwood's body slid gracefully through the opening and into the floor of the limo.

"Okay, close it, close it," I said. Xandra pressed the same button as Gregory stared up at her in utter disbelief. I turned to see Lockwood righting himself, brushing off the front of his suit. He paid no mind to the scorch marks along his left leg, or the tear in the sleeve that looked far too much like fingernail marks.

"Hello," he said, running his fingers through his dark hair.

A memory flashed across my mind of his slate blue hair and wings. It was almost as if I could see them in the limo with us. "Glad you're all right," I said.

"Get on the highway," Lockwood said, smiling tightly at me, then gracefully climbing into the driver's compartment to sit next to Gregory. "Take the next left."

"Next left?" Gregory asked. "Like that one?"

Lockwood groaned. "Yes. That one that you ignored completely. All right, take the *next* left."

"How far behind were the vampires?" I asked, my heart still keeping its frantic pace.

Lockwood turned and looked at Mill. I saw a crease form between his brow. He spotted the red blood, too.

"Not sure," Lockwood said.

"You flew all the way here?" Derrick asked.

Lockwood flashed a mischievous grin that I hadn't seen in some time. "It's one of my many charms."

Iona groaned from the back seat.

"How is she?" Lockwood asked.

"I'm not sure–" I started.

"She'll be fine," Mill said.

I glared at him.

"She will," he said. "She just needs to eat. Blood heals."

I turned away.

Gregory let out another yelp from the front seat.

"Turn right, *right*," Lockwood cut in. "At this light. *Now*."

I looked over at Iona, not convinced that she was fine. Her face was a shade of gray that I had never seen, and all the veins on the back of her hands were standing out prominently. There were silvery circles under her eyes as if she had been painted in shimmery eyeshadow. I wasn't entirely convinced that Mill wasn't just telling me what I wanted to hear as a way for making me feel better about what he did.

My stomach turned over again as I looked away.

"The highway!" Gregory said, whooping. "I did it!"

"Excellent. Now move over," Lockwood said. "I'll take it from here."

There was a horrible, jolting *crash* that reverberated throughout the limo. It stopped moving, but I didn't.

I slammed against the seat, my neck crumpling beneath my own weight pressing against it. There was another sudden weight against me as someone else smashed into me.

"I swear that wasn't my fault!" Gregory yelled.

"What – what just happened–" Xandra said.

"Someone just tried to run us off the road," Lockwood said thinly. "I believe your vampire friends have...caught us."

24

"Gregory, step on it," Lockwood said. He was still in the passenger seat, though he looked about ready to physically move Gregory out of the way. My heart skipped a beat as I heard the strain in his voice. He had been ready to shift seats when the limo had been struck, and he'd been thrown into the floor of the passenger seat. Silver blood gleamed at the back of his head where he'd struck. Fortunately, the air bags hadn't deployed, or they might have broken his neck. Now he was trying to draw himself back up, his face screwed up in pain.

"It's all right, Iona, it's fine," Laura was saying, her face having lost all color. There were streaks of black blood all over the floor.

"You know, when limos like this crash, they have a higher fatality rate than a normal car crash," Gregory called from the front seat.

"Thank you, Mr. Statistic, but could you just concentrate on *not running us off the road?*" Xandra shouted.

"It's because no one wears a seatbelt in these things," Gregory babbled on, voice thin, high, and nervous as he jacked the wheel to the right. "It's like they think they're invincible."

"I'm not feeling invincible right now," Laura said, dusting off as she pulled herself back up onto the back seat. "I'm actually feeling quite vincible." She looked at Derrick. "Is 'vincible' a word? It should be."

"I think 'vulnerable' covers it," Derrick said softly.

The limo was filled with clicks as everyone found the nearest seatbelt and fastened in. The high whine of the engine and the blurring scenery outside the windows showed that we were back up to speed, and none of us wanted to repeat the last, sudden impact.

"Hard left, Gregory, hard left," Lockwood said, bracing himself against the dashboard. "They've got cars to our right.

Gregory obeyed, but it wasn't without a shriek in a higher register than I could hit myself.

"There's more on the right," Mill said from the other window.

"How are we going to outrun them in this pig?" I asked, drawing a very hurt look from Lockwood. "Sorry."

"Let us not panic," Lockwood said. "I know this city better than anyone. Stay on the highway."

"That's crazy," Gregory said. "They're right there, and they're going to–"

SLAM!

"Probably don't need to tell you, but that was the car that struck us the first time," Mill said. Out his window, I could see a muscle car that looked like it was straight out of the seventies, with a finish that had probably been quite nice before the driver started using it as a battering ram.

"If they hit us any harder, they are going to cause us to

spin out," Lockwood said. "Gregory, open the sunroof again. I'll see what sorts of spells I can scrounge up."

"But you've got to be exhausted," I said. "You don't need–"

"As of right this minute, I am the only defense," Lockwood said. "Unless any of you happen to be carrying Super Soakers loaded with holy water?" He glanced around perfunctorily. "I thought not. Gregory, open the sunroof." And he slid past me into the passenger compartment.

Gregory's hand slapped the roof of the car as he tried hard to keep the limo between the lanes with his other. Eventually he struck the right one, and the sunroof slid open.

Lockwood stood, the top half of his body sticking out of the limo like a drunk prom attendee. But instead of glowsticks and cheap beer in his hands, he sent brilliant orbs of magic in the direction of the cars pursuing us. That seventies ride suffered a tire blowout and skidded out, receding behind us in the distance.

"Yes!" I pumped my fist. Lockwood for the win. As always.

"Cassie..." I looked over at Laura, and she lifted her hand from Iona's back, and it was coated in slick, black blood.

"She needs blood," Mill said. "Soon."

"Don't look at me," Xandra said, folding her arms over her chest. "I'm not a walking, talking blood bag."

"Wasn't suggesting that," Mill said tightly. The red stains on his face gave him a sinister air, and I shuddered, looking away.

Lockwood ducked back inside, and the knot around my heart tightened. He brought in the smell of the summer air with him, the humid, salty scent of the bay. "Well, that's one of them. They've backed up traffic, which is only going to help us."

"How many are still in pursuit?" Mill asked.

"Three," he said. "And they are doing a marvelous job dodging in and out of traffic. I can't get a decent shot at them."

"Lockwood, do you have any blood?" Laura asked. "Iona – she really needs it."

Lockwood looked crestfallen, rubbing his wrists. There were green scorch marks on his palms. I didn't know exactly what that meant, but it didn't strike me as a good thing. Neither did his somewhat pale demeanor. "In fact I don't," he said. "I brought some along, but unfortunately it was left behind in the retreat from the restaurant." He gave me a sad sort of smile before standing up out of the sunroof again.

"There's gotta be something we can do," Xandra said. "Lockwood is carrying all the freight."

"Don't forget me!" Gregory called. "I'm drivi – hooooly crap, get out of the way!" He laid on the horn. There was a car in front of us traveling at grandma speed in the left lane. I saw a familiar silhouette in the window, leering back at me–

Jacquelyn.

My eyes widened, and time seemed to slow. "Gregory! That's them!"

"What?" Sure enough, the car in front of us slammed on their brakes. Gregory shrieked again, and managed to throw the limo out of the reach of the car in front. The whole limo lurched, skidding, threatening to upheave onto its side.

As we hurtled by the vamp's car, a ball of brilliant blue light struck the side of it. Sparks like bolts of lightning snaked over the hood, the top, the trunk. It stopped moving, and Lockwood let out a cry of success.

"Yes! Two down!" Xandra shouted. I saw Jacquelyn's grim face as we went by; she sure didn't look injured, though the car was coming to a slow, gliding stop.

"Are we actually gonna pull this off?" Derrick asked, staring up Lockwood.

Lockwood leaned back in. "Gregory, get all the way to the right-hand lane."

"That's the exit only lane," he replied.

"Yes, but I won't get a clear shot otherwise."

Gregory grumbled, but he slowly made his way over to the right lane.

My heart was racing. Iona was growing more statue-like with every second, more of her blood dripping out onto the seat and then the floor, staining the carpet. Xandra was biting down on her thumbnail, staring out of the windshield in the front of the limo. Laura was looking at Iona with a worry line in her forehead. She kept glancing up at me. Neither of us were really sure what was going to happen. Without blood, she wasn't healing like vampires normally did.

After a moment, Lockwood sunk down into the limo again, making Xandra and I jump.

"What's going on?" Derrick asked. "Are they still following?"

"Not anymore," Lockwood said. He was breathing heavily, dabbing at his forehead with his sleeve. "Gregory, take the exit, then the next left. Let's make sure that we really lose them once and for all."

Gregory let out a massive sigh of relief. "Oh, thank God. I thought we were gonna die. I thought I would hit a streetlamp or something, or–"

"Don't get complacent now," Lockwood said. "You need to get us off this highway."

I heard the sound of an ambulance in the distance, and I worried about all of those people that we left behind, defenseless. Would those vampires have hung around and fed? How many were actually doing Jacquelyn's bidding, and weren't just doing this for the fun of it, the chance to snag some blood in the chaos she perpetrated?

We had evaded the vampires. For now.

But what was the cost of it?

Xandra, Derrick, Laura, and Gregory were safe. So was Lockwood.

But Iona. She struggled, and the uncertainty plagued me like a thorn in my side.

And that man that Mill had been feeding on...

Did he have a wife? Kids?

All I could imagine was what their night would be like when they got the phone call telling them that they found his body outside of the restaurant...dead.

25

"Everyone okay?" I asked, looking around the inside of the limo. Nods all around were my answer, my crew stoic and injured. The whole limo smelled of blood, of sweat, and fatigue. The cushion was soft against my back, and I brushed my hands against the smooth cloth and then my dress, discovering rips and tears I hadn't even noticed until now. I looked at Lockwood, who had settled down in the seat beside Derrick. It was clear that he was worn out. There were beads of sweat at his temples, and his cheeks had a sallow look to them. "What about you?" I said to him. "Are you all right?"

Lockwood nodded, wiping his brow with a flawless handkerchief he produced from the front of his jacket.

Derrick arched a brow as he watched Lockwood dab his face.

"What?" Lockwood retorted. "Can't a man have a nice handkerchief for stressful situations?"

"The last person I ever saw use one of those was my grandpa," Derrick said.

Lockwood sighed rather dramatically, putting the handkerchief away as delicately as he had pulled it out.

"Are the vampires gone?" Xandra asked, turning in her seat beside me to look out the front window. "Like, they aren't gonna affix themselves to our window like those little sticky plushies?"

"We are safe," Lockwood said. "At least for the time being. Though I do not think they will waste very much time in coming after us again."

My stomach gave an uncomfortable lurch. That was the opposite of what I wanted to hear.

"What was that chick's problem?" Xandra asked, looking at me, shaking her head. "I mean, I get that she hates your guts...but this seemed a little OTT, y'know?"

"What does OTT mean?" Mill asked, his heavy brow furrowed.

"I know," I said. "They just...ambushed us on the street. I'm used to being attacked at inconvenient times, but the fact that they did it in public, with all of those witnesses...and the body count."

Lockwood's brow furrowed.

"Guys, where am I going?" Gregory called from the front. "I'm literally just driving around right now."

"Shut up, Gregory, the adults are talking," Xandra said. "And it's 'over the top.'"

"Oh," Mill said. "That makes sense."

"I think that is the most troubling part of it all," Lockwood said, scratching his chin. "It has been a very long time since I have seen vampires attack so openly before."

Mill arched an eyebrow. "I haven't seen it at all in my time, Lockwood. Especially not in the States."

"You are aware, then, of the 1895 riots in London?" Lockwood asked.

"You were there?" Mill asked, incredulous. "You never told me–"

"This is not the time for a stroll down memory lane," I said, shooting Mill a dirty look. "What does it mean, that they just attacked like they did?"

"Duh, obvious," Xandra said. "Jacquelyn really hates you."

"This is more than mere pique," Lockwood said. "It was planned. They've been watching us."

"Oh, great," I said, sinking back against the seat. "Just what I needed. More vampire stalkers."

"It's even worse when it's your ex-bestie," Xandra said. "Man, she's pretty obsessed, isn't she?"

"That's kind of what happens when you become consumed with revenge," Derrick said. "It just...becomes all-consuming." He was running his fingers over a scar on the back of his hand, silvery in the light of the neon strips running around the ceiling of the limo. It made me wonder if it was a reminder of the night his dad had finally snapped.

"Lucky we had Iona and Mill with us," Laura said, her voice quiet. "Can you imagine if they hadn't been?"

"Maybe Jacquelyn thought we would be alone," I said.

"She didn't seem exactly upset about the fact that they were with us, though," Laura said. "Look what she did to Iona..."

"Uncomfortable question," Xandra said. "We can't go home now, can we?"

"No," Lockwood said. "It is likely that Jacquelyn will have found out where all of your houses are, if she didn't know already."

"She definitely will," I said.

"This must have taken months of preparations," Xandra said.

"She hit us right where we live," Derrick said. "Came after us just like she did that day on the beach."

I frowned. He was right. She wasn't exactly coming after me, was she? She was coming after those I cared about. There were countless times that she could have lashed out and hurt me that night, but she didn't. Because she knew that making me watch those other people suffer was more painful for me.

My stomach plummeted.

"Gregory, get back to my house. Now."

"What?" He turned, looking over the seat. "Why?"

"My parents." The answer almost hurt to speak aloud. "She's going to go after my parents."

26

We had only moved back into our real house about a month ago. All of the walls had been freshly painted, and somehow they had managed to get rid of any trace of the smoky smell from the fire. Mom insisted that she wanted a bay window where the original dining room window had been, since it had been smashed to bits. Most of the second story was untouched, but there had been a lot of concern about the structural integrity of the house because of the fire. And they only asked one question about the smashed back door where I had kicked the vampire through. It was awfully...body shaped.

A limo in the middle of a suburban neighborhood wasn't exactly what you would call discreet. It had been a few hours since we had left for the play, so it wasn't like it was weird that we were coming back to the house.

What was weird, though, was that when I jumped out of the limo before Gregory had even put it in park, I saw the front door was wide open.

The front door. Mom and Dad never used the front door. The sprinklers next door were going, their repetitive hissing breaking the silence of the night. A gentle breeze brushed across my sweating face, making my hair stick to my temples. I brushed it away from my eyes.

"Oh, crap," Xandra said as she crawled out of the limo behind me.

I lingered on the sidewalk. I should go in. I knew I should, but this was all far too familiar, too similar.

"What's the matter?" Derrick asked, getting out.

All of the color had drained from my face, but I didn't have any adrenaline left to pump through my body. I swallowed nervously, but balled my hands into fists, and started toward the door.

"Cassie, wait," Xandra said, hurrying to keep up. "What if the vampires are still in here? We should go in carefully–"

"I hope they are," I said, brandishing my stake, still coated with black vamp ichor. "So I can kill them myself. I am tired of them picking on my parents." I used my foot to push the door open, and Xandra and Derrick followed in after me.

As soon as I crossed over the threshold, I heard voices. Crouching down, I pressed my finger to my lips in Derrick and Xandra's direction. They nodded their heads as we continued on.

The entrance way was quiet. The rug in the front hall was slightly askew, the bottom right corner overturned as if someone had tripped over it. I continued down the hall as quietly as a vampire would, walking passed the dining room, and ending up in the kitchen.

The lights over the island were on, but the living room beyond was dark aside from the light from the television. Mom and Dad must have been binging on an early season of *Frasier*. He and his brother were shouting at each other about something, with the audience's laughter following along afterwards.

The remains of two ceramic mugs were spread on the floor of the kitchen, shattered. My heart lurched as I realized they were two of Mom's favorites; handmade from grandma's workshop. The faucet in the sink was running, the water swirling around the basin of the sink before sinking down into the drain.

A side table beside the couch had been toppled over. There was a burning smell coming from the oven. When I pulled it open, I saw what were probably cookies at one point in time. Smoke billowed out, threatening to choke me as I hit the kill switch to turn off the oven. I was lucky the house hadn't caught on fire again. I hastily – and quietly – cracked the door to allow the heat to escape faster.

"I don't think the vampires are here," I said, fanning the smoke out. "They would have attacked by now. There's no reason for them to be scared of us."

"Speak for yourself," Xandra said with a wink.

Derrick had wandered into the living room, stooping to pick up the end table. "There's a lamp over here with a shattered bulb."

"Looks like there are some groceries over here?" Xandra said. "Non-perishables, though."

"Dad was putting those away before we left," I said. I sank down on one of the barstools at the island, trying really hard to keep myself from freaking out.

Again. This happened again. How many times would I leave my parents alone before I realized that I couldn't do that without them getting kidnapped by vampires? What a role reversal we had in our family; instead of the parents worrying about their wayward daughter getting kidnapped, I had to worry about them.

"Miss Cassandra?" Lockwood was standing just inside the back door.

"What?" I asked, slowly getting to my feet. He'd circled around the house while the three of us came in the front.

"Cassie?" My mom peered out from behind Lockwood, her hair looking a bit mussed and a leaf sticking from her shirt, but otherwise none the worse for the wear. Dad was a step behind.

My heart swelled with relief as I hurried over to them, throwing my arms around both of their necks at once. "Oh, my God, I am so glad that you're okay. What happened?" I asked, pulling away from them.

Dad adjusted his glasses. "Vampires," he muttered.

"Mill and I did a search of the whole perimeter of the house, and didn't see any evidence of vampires," Lockwood said. "What happened?"

Dad scratched the back of his neck. "They got here about an hour and a half after you left. Came right in through the front door; I guess I forgot to lock it after you all left for the play."

"But how did you manage to escape them?" I asked.

"We heard them coming and snuck out through the garage," Dad said. "I don't think they realized that we were home. They were...not quiet."

"Very impressive," Lockwood said. "Your instincts told you that something was wrong."

"Where did you hide?" I asked.

"Just out back," Dad said. "In the bushes."

"How long were you sitting outside?" Xandra asked, looking him over. He did look like he'd been hiding in the bushes a while. His pants bore serious dirt stains all around the knees and backside.

"I don't even know what time it is," Dad said, looking at the clock over the oven. "An hour? Maybe more?"

"They were trying to sweep in while we were preoccupied," Lockwood said.

"Wait, hang on a second," I said, turning to Dad. "Why in the world didn't you call us?"

Dad's face flushed. "We didn't have our phones on us."

Sure enough, when I looked behind me, I saw his and Mom's phone chargers plugged in on the kitchen counter like they were every night. But their phones were gone.

"They took your phones," I said, frowning. "They really didn't want you to be able to get ahold of me."

"When did they leave?" Lockwood asked.

"No idea," Dad said. He turned and looked at me. "What's going on, Cass? I thought you said that all of this vampire nonsense was over."

"I thought it was," I said. "But...Jacquelyn showed herself again tonight."

"Jacquelyn?" Mom had straightened up, the dustpan and broom in her hands, the chunks of broken mug gathered in a neat pile on the floor. "I thought that she had been...dealt with." Mom's voice went hushed.

"Um...you mean 'staked?' No." A lump formed in my throat. "She was at the meeting that I had with Lord Varycas."

Mom cocked her head to the side. "You could have mentioned that."

I sighed. "I thought we had a deal. Found out the hard way tonight that we don't. And she knows where I live, so this place isn't safe anymore."

"If they were coming after your parents, it is likely that they are not done threatening us," Lockwood said.

"If they think they can get away with breaking my stuff, and so soon after moving back in, they've got another think coming," Mom said as she tipped the dust bin into the trash. "I loved those mugs."

"Priorities, Mom," I said. "We need to get out of here."

"Agreed," Lockwood said. "It is possible they have left watchers somewhere in the neighborhood."

That thought made my skin crawl. What if they were watching us right now, seeing us through the windows, waiting to make their move on us as soon as our backs were turned?

"We need to go," I said. "Mom, Dad, get whatever you think you'll need and let's move."

Mom gave Dad a look. "We just got back into this house. Do we really have to leave?"

"It's not forever," he said soothingly.

I certainly hoped it wasn't.

We grabbed clothes, toiletries, camping gear, food and the like. We had no idea where we were going or how long we would be gone for, but we packed as quickly and as comprehensively as a five-minute time limit allowed, and then we were out the door.

As Dad turned the key in the lock, my heart sank. There was a sort of finality to it that made my skin crawl.

"Onward?" Lockwood asked me with a resigned smile.

"And upward," I said. Together we walked down the sidewalk, to the limo, and on to an uncertain future.

27

The smell in the limo was...less than appealing when we crawled back inside. In the heat of the getaway, none of us had noticed the pungent tang of the vampire blood. Mom covered her nose as she crawled inside, and Dad's face turned a shade of green.

"Oh my gosh, your parents are okay," Laura exclaimed, her eyes wide as she watched them settle into the seats beside me. The car door opened up front beside the driver's side.

"Whoa, hey now, what are you– " Gregory started. Lockwood's grabbed his shoulder and yanked him out. He then proceeded to slide into the driver's seat, adjusting the front of his lapel.

The back door opened and Gregory crawled inside, muttering under his breath. "I could have driven. I was finally getting the hang of it."

"She...doesn't look so good," Mom said, looking over at Iona who was stretched across one of the side seats. While we had been inside, Laura had taken the opportunity to adjust her so she was flat on her back.

"She's still unconscious," Laura said, running fingers through Iona's pale hair.

Mill sat off to the side, his arms crossed. "She's sleeping, trying to conserve her strength."

"What do we do?" Gregory asked. "We can't exactly take her to a hospital."

I cocked my head, looking at my dad. "No, we can't. But we could...sort of bring the hospital to her."

My dad nodded, slowly, then started to roll up his sleeves as he crouched his way across the limo to take a look at her. There were occasions when having a doctor for a father was useful.

"Where are we headed?" Lockwood asked from the front, adjusting the rearview mirror.

I looked over at Laura and Gregory. "If they hit my house, they are definitely going to hit yours."

Laura nodded her head. "I thought so, too. But Gregory and I were looking while you guys were inside. Our houses seem completely fine."

"We should drive by, just to make sure," I said, looking back up at Lockwood.

Lockwood eased the limo away from the sidewalk. We made our way down the street, everyone craning their necks to peer outside the windows.

"See? My house looks fine," Gregory said. "My parents are visiting my aunt and uncle near Orlando for the night. Going to Disney Springs or something."

"And you didn't invite us all to a raucous house party?" Xandra asked with mock offense.

"My parents are out of town, too," Laura said as we passed by her house. "So it shouldn't look like anyone was there after I left this afternoon."

"I say again," Xandra said. "You are all such a disappointment to me. The Beastie Boys fought for your right to party and you all go see a play." She made a mock disgusted noise deep in her throat. "Shame. Shame."

I chewed on the inside of my lip. "If they have been watching our houses all day, then what in the world are we supposed to do?"

"Not go home, for starters," Mill said. "At least not until this has all been dealt with."

"I agree with Mr. Mill," Lockwood said.

"But I don't think they hit either of their houses," Xandra said, shaking her head. "I mean, it was pretty clear when we pulled up they had hit yours. And the inside was tossed. They weren't exactly subtle, were they?"

"I think it would have been a lot more obvious," Lockwood agreed.

"Our house. Why is it always our house?" Mom muttered, folding her arms over her chest.

"Because our daughter decided to embrace vampire slaying as a curative to her compulsive lying," my dad said, his hands covered in Iona's black ichor. He shot me an embarrassed look. "Sorry."

"No, it's true," I said, still feeling a little stung. "What about Xandra's house? Let's go check it out."

A few minutes later, we found there was no damage to the exterior of Xandra's house either. "My mom's gone visiting family, so Dad's been working late," she said. "Makes sense that he isn't home yet. His car's not in the driveway."

"Does Jacquelyn not know as much about everyone as I thought?" I asked. "Because it seems obvious she would have attacked your houses too, right?"

Xandra shook her head. "No. *You're* the target, Cass. She

doesn't care about our parents or our stuff. She cares about getting to the people who are important to *you*."

Oh. Well. That was just *great*. Mom and Dad gave me uneasy looks, but I did my best to keep my face blank. She had a point; I sighed heavily, glaring out the window. "You're probably right. Everything involving Jacquelyn is always about me. About how I ruined her life. How I took everything from her. She never forgave me."

Gregory gave a loud snort. "That much is obvious." He recoiled into his seat when he caught glares from Laura and Xandra. "Uh...I mean..."

"But how far is she willing to take this?" I wondered aloud. "She's the one who broke the peace, coming at us in public like that."

"One thing's for sure...this is not going to stay quiet," Xandra went on. "The human community and vamp community are going to be all over this mess."

"Yeah, but the local news stations aren't going to report them as vampire attacks," Gregory said. "Maybe as some kind of gang violence."

"Regardless, who knows what she is gonna try and pull next?" I asked. "That's the real worry.

"So...we're going to have to be ready for another fight," Gregory said.

I looked around the car; Iona was still bleeding on the seat, though Dad seemed to be staunching her wounds. Mom was staring at me with wide eyes. Derrick was looking out the window, lost in his own thoughts. Mill was trying hard to meet my eye, but I avoided his gaze, as well as the crimson-caked ring around his mouth.

"We're going to need to stop, somewhere we can offload some of the noncombatants," I said. "They need to hide, or we're not going to be able to fight."

"Yeah, but where?" Xandra asked. "All of our houses could be at least watched by vamps."

"Mine definitely will be," Mill said. "As would Iona's."

"What about Byron's?" Gregory asked. "Wasn't that just abandoned after your fight with the witches there?"

"Too risky," Lockwood said. "Draven could have easily told Jacquelyn where it was during her time with him."

I bit down on my thumbnail. "Where can we go?"

Lockwood glanced up at us all in the rearview mirror. "I may be able to provide a place."

28

Lockwood pulled the limo up to the curb in a quiet neighborhood a little farther north of where I lived. It was a pleasant neighborhood, with a lot of old Florida houses, all single story, and a large park across the street with an enormous red, yellow, and blue playground, a soccer field, and a pond perfect for lazy afternoons of bird watching. Though there wouldn't be much bird watching in the middle of the night by the light of the street lamps.

The hot, sticky humidity clung to my skin, making sweat glisten above my lip and seep into the back of my shirt. I hoped that wherever Lockwood was taking us had air conditioning. "Where are we?" I whispered. Everyone seemed to be walking really quietly, careful to not even step off the sidewalk into the Bermuda grass.

"Home," Lockwood said with a small smile.

He led the way up the path to a little blue house with white shutters and a tin roof. A mailbox in the shape of a dolphin sat out beside the sidewalk, and a pair of rocking chairs sat on the little front porch as we stepped up to the front door.

"This is your place?" Gregory said. "Gotta admit, I was expecting...more?"

Lockwood said nothing, simply producing a key out of thin air – thank you, magic – and slid it home in the lock. When he pushed the door open, my jaw fell open, because across the threshold was something that looked far more like Faerie than Earth.

Oh my gosh, *maaagic*.

There was greenery everywhere. The walls were draped in snaking ivy, ferns with leaves the size of hubcaps, and flowering branches that intertwined and crawled across the ceiling. The air was much less warm, with a pleasant, gentle scent of lavender.

"Um, Lockwood, where are we?" I asked.

"Still in Tampa," he said, closing the door behind Mom and Dad, who had come through the door last. "This is just a little upgrade that I have given to the house."

"I have to admit, faeries are pretty cool," Xandra said. "Is this what it was like when you were there?"

I nodded. "Pretty much, yeah. Lots of green everything."

"Wow..." she muttered, wandering farther in.

Laura was beaming. I had seen plenty of animations where characters' eyes sparkled, but I had never seen it in real life. "Are these all from Faerie?" she asked. She reached out and gently touched a bright pink flower with enormous round petals. It was humming softly.

Lockwood nodded. "I find it best to have a piece of home with me wherever I go."

She dashed over to a wooden table that seemed to be made of the roots of a tree. "And these?" There were tiny glass vials and mortar and pestles resting there. Some sort of powder was glowing from within the bowl.

"Just some alchemy," he said nonchalantly.

Laura was positively bursting with excitement as she wandered around the room.

"Here," Lockwood said, indicating a wooden log that was as tall as his waist, but it was carved into the shape of a long bench. He snapped his fingers and lush, red cushions appeared, falling gently onto the bench.

Mill walked over, seemingly unburdened by his...well, burden, and eased Iona down onto the cushions.

"We'll be safe here, right?" I asked.

"As long as no one followed us, then most certainly," Lockwood said. "I keep a close watch on my street for any sign of watchers. There has been no hint of them."

"How do you do that?" Gregory asked. Then, a moment later, the answer occurred to him. "Magic?"

"Magic," Lockwood agreed.

"Good," I said, heaving a sigh of relief.

"Do you have a first aid kit?" my dad asked Lockwood. He was kneeling next to Iona, and a moment later, pads sprouted beneath his knees, and a chair of pure, white wood appeared next to him as if it had sprouted from the earthy floor. With another snap of Lockwood's fingers, a bright red metal case appeared next to Dad. When he caught me staring, Lockwood answered me with a shrug. "I thought it best to keep medical supplies around for humans just in case of situations like this." He frowned. "Though I never believed we would need to come here."

"It's like being back in Faerie," I told him. "You know, without the people trying to kill us with their internecine wars."

He gave me a small smile. "I thought that you might appreciate it."

Dad snapped on a pair of gloves and started peeling away the fabric of Iona's dress from around the wound.

"Cassie, could you hand me some of those antiseptic pads?"

I tore them open and handed them to him. "How is this going to help? She's not exactly alive."

"I'm cleaning the wound, just like with any other patient," he said.

Just then, I heard a groan of discomfort and looked up to see Iona opening her eyes. It took a second for the fog to clear as she registered what was happening. She blinked a few times, her gaze sharpening, her eyes widening. "Um...hi everyone?" Her bright eyes went wide as she looked around. "Why are we in an enchanted forest?"

I heard Laura squeal with delight from somewhere in a different...room? Did this place have rooms?

"Miss Laura, please do not touch the rabbits, for they are not, in fact, rabbits, and you will have the most unpleasant experience if one of them were to bite you," Lockwood called over his shoulder. I could see a tightness in his eyes.

"My home is the safest place for us all for the time being," Lockwood said gently. "It's nothing to be worried about."

Iona's face screwed up in pain as Dad pressed her stomach wound. I didn't even recall seeing her get it in all the melee.

"Yeah, that's not good." He looked up at me. "She needs blood."

"Yeah, no kidding," Iona said, her head sinking back down onto the squishy cushion. "Like, now would be great."

"I have some," Lockwood said. "Would you prefer AB positive, or O negative?"

"I do not care," Iona said. "I'd drink it straight out of a mosquito right now."

"Glad to see you haven't lost your sense of humor," I told her.

Lockwood disappeared and reappeared in a flash. "Here you are," he said. He had put a purple bendy straw in the hole of the blood bag where the medical tube would normally have gone. Like it was a Capri-Sun.

Iona clasped her lips around the straw and started sucking on it as if she had never had a drink before in her life. My stomach turned over and I had to look away. She finished it with one more gulp, tossed it to the floor, and made an, "Ahhhhh," sound like she'd just had the most satisfying beverage ever. Then she collapsed, resting her head back against the cushions. "That hit the spot." She pointed at the gaping wound in her belly.

"Whoa," Dad said, jerking his hands back from the wound. It was crusting over rapidly, the black goo solidifying like burnt cheese drippings left in the bottom of a piping hot oven. A few seconds later, it was done, and Dad gently probed the crust. It flaked off at the edge, and beneath was flawless – incredibly pale – skin where the wound had been moments before.

"Looks like my work here is done," Dad said, brushing a little more of the ashy crust off to reveal more skin. "I'm going to go check on your mother," Dad said, giving me a pat on the shoulder.

"Thanks," Iona said casually, pulling her dress back down. Like now she was concerned about her modesty or something. "Good thing we both didn't need one, huh?" Iona said, turning cold eyes to Mill. "Of course, I guess we would have if you hadn't decided to feed on roadkill."

My heart skipped a beat. So it wasn't just me who thought what he did was totally out of line. I was suddenly even more appreciative of Iona. She was on my side with this.

"I did what I had to do," Mill said. There was a tightness in his words.

"Yeah, that so doesn't justify it," Iona said, laying back. "We're better than them, Mill. Or at least I am."

"And look where you ended up." Mill's face was tight, his voice like a tiger in a cage. "On a couch with only a bag of blood. You'll still need hours for that wound to finish healing."

"Better than helping Jacquelyn's clan finish what they started, slaughtering the innocent," Iona spat back.

My heart was like a kettle set over the coals. It was bubbling, churning, sputtering. Any more and it was sure to burst out. But this was not the time for this discussion. With enormous effort, I shoved away my anger, and stepped up between them. "Our concern right now is what we need to do next," I said. "We can't just hide here in Lockwood's place for the rest of our lives."

"I could," came Laura's voice. She was holding a bright blue book, or rather, the book was trying to hold her. She seemed not to notice the pages trying to crawl up her hand, like they were caught in some unseen breeze.

"Come now, Miss Laura," Lockwood said, hurrying over to her. He grabbed the book from her hands, shutting it heavily. "Allow me to show you something that won't try to hurt you." He guided her around a tree trunk, a look of great patience upon his face.

"I saw the hate in Jacquelyn's eyes," I said. "She is not going to hold off for long."

"She's always been like that, though, hasn't she?" Mom was drumming her fingers anxiously on her arms.

"What do you mean?" I asked.

"When you were kids, she always wanted to be the first to soccer practice during the summer. Always impatient while we were getting ready to take you to the mall or to a movie. Even when she was in school, she never did well sitting in her desk after tests, or during lectures. She just always had to be moving toward the next thing."

"Vampirism just makes you more of what you already are," Iona said softly. "It gives amplified voice to the id within."

"So she's become more of all that, then," I said. My heart sank, the familiar guilt washing over me. The reality that this was entirely my fault hit me square on the nose, making me sick to my stomach.

"She's a big girl and is more than capable of making her own decisions," Xandra said. She had reappeared with a bright blue flower behind her ear, not unlike the shade of her hair. "Just because she blames you for everything doesn't mean that she's immune from the consequences. You didn't tell her to turn all psycho and start killing people, not in New York and certainly not down here."

"What consequences, though?" I said. "She's not been punished once for her actions. If anything, she's honored for them. She's had the ear of two different vampire Lords now. I mean, that beats the hell out of what most teenagers have for influence. I mean...that's kind of a glow up, actually. Like a reward."

"She won't always be," Xandra said. "One day, it's gonna all come back around. Just you wait."

"Yeah, well, I hope that day is today," I said. "I don't think I can really deal with any of this anymore."

"She wasn't the brightest girl, though, was she?" Dad said. "She always looked up to you for your grades and your intelligence. I think she just always wanted to be accepted, and she admired you and loved that you gave her the time of day." He hesitated. "Y'know...until..."

I frowned. "Until my constant lying came back to bite me in the butt?" I swear, I was going to be paying for that for the rest of my life. Which might end soon, and it'd all be my fault, really.

"So what's the plan?" Gregory asked, stepping up to the group.

"We're trying to figure that out," I said. "We have to do something."

"Jacquelyn cannot go unchecked like this," Xandra said. "I think that needs to be our primary focus."

"She's right," Lockwood agreed. "If she continues on like this, the body count is only going to grow."

"She seems insistent," Iona said from the couch. "I don't think she is going to back down any time soon."

"Then we need help," I said. "We need to put Jacquelyn in check. And the only way we can do that is if we go to the top."

"Cassie, you don't mean–" Xandra said.

"I do," I said. "We need to go see Lord Varycas."

"But why?" Gregory asked. "Wasn't his advisor there tonight?" He looked around. "Doesn't that mean the peace is over?"

"Maybe, maybe not," I said. "Jacquelyn said that she was doing what she wanted. If she didn't have permission to do what she just did, then I still have the protection of the Lord of Tampa."

Mill was frowning. "You want to wager your life on that?"

"He could have killed us last time we visited," I said. "Easily. He didn't. What's changed in the last couple months? Why spring a kill trap on us tonight when he could have done it then?" I shook my head. "This is all Jacquelyn. She waited until she had enough force, and then she moved."

"Operating from that premise, it would be best to resolve this before it goes any further," Lockwood said. "If you are going to stick your head in the lion's mouth, best to do it sooner, rather than later."

"Uh, no," Gregory said. "Later would be better. Like, after you've had a long, full life, and your supermodel has lost her looks and her lustiness." He caught a few glares. "What? I can't be the only one thinking I don't want to die yet. I have my whole life ahead of me."

"Let me read your future for you," Xandra said, putting a hand on Gregory's head and closing her eyes. "There are no supermodels in your future. And probably no lustiness, either."

"Really not feeling the love in here," Gregory said, pushing her hand away roughly.

"Nor anywhere else," Xandra said. "Because of the lack of lustiness, see?"

"If we try to meet with Varycas, he's going to think we're too presumptuous," Mill said, pinching the bridge of his nose. "Lords do not like being interrupted by people like us. Especially not humans."

"Do we really have another option, though?" I asked.

When I got nothing in response but long faces, I sighed.

"Then to Varycas we go," I said. "Or I do, at least."

"I will go with you," Lockwood said.

"Varycas is not going to agree to a party reservation," Mill said. "And the last thing you want to do is march more of your friends into his clutches if by chance he's in on this."

"Agreed," I said, then looked around at my friends. "I

need to go alone." I looked right at Lockwood. "You can't go. You need to stay here and protect the others."

"Another youthful suicide," Gregory said. "I'm really going to miss you, Cassie. Though I am wondering where those brains are that Jacquelyn admired you for." I ignored him; bravery sometimes required stupidity.

"I'll go with you," Mill said. "I am not going to let you walk into his place all alone."

Anger bubbled inside of me as I glared at him. I would have much preferred that I was going with Iona instead, but she was laid up. Varycas didn't know any of the others, so they couldn't come.

"Fine, then," I said. "Mill and me."

Mom gave me a stern look. "The only reason why I am letting you leave this...this house...is because I know that Mill will be with you."

A nasty bitterness rose in my throat. "I'll be fine, Mom. Really."

"You always say that," she said. "And yet, here I am, still worrying like a mother does."

"What about a stake?" Laura asked. She hurried over and pressed a fresh stake into my hands. She beamed. "I found an extra in the bottom of my purse. Hopefully you won't have to use it."

"And perhaps a change of attire is in order," Lockwood said, returning with bottles of water.

He snapped his fingers, and my clothes immediately changed. My tattered dress was gone, replaced with dark blue jeans, a pair of tennis shoes, and my favorite blue T-shirt with the pocket in the front.

"Thanks, Lockwood," I said. It even smelled like they had been freshly washed in my favorite detergent. It gave me a small boost of confidence to be wearing something more comfortable, more...me.

And Varycas probably wouldn't have taken kindly to us showing up at his doorsteps, covered in blood. Like ringing the dinner bell or something. "Let's go," I said to Mill. "No point wasting any more time. Let's get this over with."

29

Lockwood's limo was awfully quiet. It was amazing how much bigger it felt, even up in the front seat like I was, when there was no one else inside of it. Since it was the only vehicle at our disposal, Lockwood insisted that we take it. So we did. That's why we were sitting there in silence, both staring straight ahead, all too aware of the prickly quiet between us now that we were alone.

"How do you know where Varycas is?" I asked. "Have you been to one of his parties? Like you used to with Draven?"

Mill's jaw clenched, his hands on the limo's wheel. "You know why I used to go to Draven's parties. It was to keep an eye on him and some of the other vampires there."

"I know that's what you've told me."

"I heard where he is from one of the vampires in his new circle," Mill said.

The GPS on my phone was telling me that we were only about four miles from Varycas's supposed estate. I watched the little blue dot follow the road north, the fast-food chains, banks, and pharmacies passing by. "Turn left up ahead," I said.

"I know a better route," Mill said. I watched as he ignored my direction, carrying on straight through the green light. I sighed, watching the GPS panic as it attempted to recalculate the shortest route.

"Why do you use that thing, anyway?" Mill asked. "Isn't it better to learn the area that you live in? Apps like that just make people stupid because they rely on them so heavily."

I pressed the sleep button on the side of my phone, the screen fading to black. "I have found it incredibly helpful as I've tried to learn the city and all of its surroundings," I said. "It's given me the chance to not get lost when I go some-where new."

"It's just like everything on the internet," Mill said. "Everything is so instantaneous. Can't you see the damage that it's doing to society?"

I rolled my eyes, not daring to look at him. "Okay, pre-Boomer." It was still hard for me to look at him and not be consumed with the memory of the blood dripping down his neck, staining the front of his shirt.

Mill shifted his hands uncomfortably on the steering wheel. "It's hard to cope with change. Especially watching your kind do it while vampires stay the same," he said. There was a bite to his words, a sort of revulsion that caught me off guard. "We're predators, hunting the helpless because your kind gave up the sword and the wariness in favor of being digitally connected and jaded as hell. They view you as less than. In the middle ages, they didn't have cars or cell phones, but they knew vampires and demons went bump in the night. Now..." He shook his head. "...You have all the tech and advantages in the world, but no awareness. You're a sleeping herd...which is why they call you cattle."

I narrowed my eyes and glared at him. "You and Iona seem to think that I'm brain dead or something. Yes, I realize that all the baddie vampires are out to get me because they see humans that way."

"Yes, you see it, now," Mill said. "How many of your kind don't? How many keep their heads in their phones as they walk down the street, waiting for some vampire to make them into dinner?"

"I'm sorry, is there a reason that we are talking about this?" I asked.

His eyes narrowed, and his brow furrowed. "Well, I didn't figure it was the right time to talk about the other thing."

"What other thing?" I asked, wary of whatever was about to come out of his mouth.

There was a loud *thump* from the back of the limo. We stared at one another, fear draining the color from my face.

Mill flipped the button that lowered the divider, and I pulled the stake out and readied it, turning in the seat, ready to slam it through a vampire's eyes if I had to. He'd raised it when we got in, presumably because it felt weird having that cavernous area behind us with no one there. When it slipped down, my heart leapt when I caught a glimpse of periwinkle purple hair.

"Xandra, what the hell are you doing here?" I asked.

She was against the seat right behind me, a champagne flute filled with sparkling water in her hands. She grinned at me like we were on our way to some party or something. "Yeah...you didn't think I was going to let you go on your own, did you?"

I blinked at her. "Well, yeah...I kinda did,."

She shook her head, her lavender hair swinging. "I'm your bestie. That's not how we do this."

I looked over at Mill who was glancing every few seconds back at her in the rearview mirror. "Turn around. We're taking her back."

"Oh, girl, I don't think so," Xandra said. "I did not sneak past Lockwood just to get taken back–"

"It's too late, anyway," Mill said. He sounded tense.

The limo slowed to an almost complete stop, and when I turned to look, I saw that we were parked in front of what looked like a gate at a resort. Vampire guards stood on either side of the drive, waving us in with only a glance.

I swallowed hard.

We were already here.

30

"You have to stay in here," I said to her, darkness surrounding all the windows as the limo rolled up the estate driveway.

Xandra looked at me from the back like I had lost my ever-loving mind. "Uh, no. That's crazy. I'll–"

"Like you're going to be any safer in a room full of vamps, including the Lord of the territory?"

"Yeah, but if we do have peace, what do I have to worry about?" She shrugged expansively. "And if it's war, well...I figure I'm toast eventually. Might as well go here, now, with you. Amirite?"

I glared at her as Mill continued up the drive. "No. Better that you have a long life with...what was it Gregory said? Lustiness? Models? Whatever."

"They better be male models, number one. And second...whoa," Xandra said, leaning past me to stare out the window. "Forget models and lust. I just want to live in this house."

The estate was impressive. The whole property was surrounded by a tall, white stone wall and had more land than a lot of the homes I had seen in Florida so far. The house was a mansion that looked like it belonged on MTV cribs. White washed and luxurious, something that looked more home to velvet and tufted settees than glass staircases and an infinity pool. There were a lot of windows to admire the gorgeous view of the tall trees in the yard and the lack of neighbors...but most were closed tight with hurricane shutters.

"That's clever," Xandra said, noticing the same thing I had. "Now I'll always wonder if families are away during hurricane season and taking extra precautions, or if vampires live there."

Mill pulled the car around to the front doors, the driveway encircling a stone fountain topped with a statue of dolphins, the water bubbling merrily even this late at night. A vampire guard stepped up to the door, and before I could withdraw my stake from my hair again, he opened the door and stood aside, allowing me to step out.

I looked over my shoulder at Xandra, and gave her my best Mom look. "Stay. Here."

"What's the point of hiding if they know I'm here?" she asked.

I rolled my eyes as she opened the back door and stepped out, arms up over her head.

"This way, please," said the guard who opened my door. He was dressed more like a butler than a guard, though, with coattails to boot. His shoes looked like they had been recently shined, and his accent was awfully...British.

The lawn had been recently mowed; its pungent aroma filled the air. I could also smell the salt of the Gulf on the humid breeze that rustled through the royal palms arching into the sky on either side of the driveway. The house was lit up, spilling out of the front door and the windows that weren't sealed up tight.

"You know, it's good you didn't leave me in there," Xandra whispered as we hopped up the steps to the front door. "There are vampires absolutely everywhere. I'd have been safer if you left out some meat and rang the dinner bell."

I wanted to give her a hard jab in the ribs, but it was better to appear as a cohesive group instead of the messy ragtag bunch we actually were. I was angry with my boyfriend, he seemed to be angry at me, and I was angry with my best friend who didn't seem to care in the least.

Yep. Totally cohesive.

There was a large knocker on the front of the stained wooden door, in the shape of a lion's head. I tried not to look too closely; my eyes were playing tricks on me and I thought its eyes were following me as we walked inside. The foyer could have been in a palace. The floors were polished marble tiles, the walls paneled with wood and gold-leaf wallpaper. I could smell fresh tea being brewed somewhere, and something like pine...maybe his housekeeper used it as a cleaner?

We were led up a short set of stairs that passed through what must have been a study or den of some sort. An enormous desk sat in front of one of the arched windows, flanked on either side by bookshelves stuffed to the brim, their spines all ancient and discolored from years of use. Leather chairs filled the room, and a very pretty grandfather clock went *tick, tock* on the far wall.

"Here you are," said the butler, or who I assumed was the butler, since he was showing us around like a butler would. "Lord Varycas will see you out here."

We stepped out onto a porch that looked more like the

terrace of a palace. It was a story up, but below I could see a huge pool that looked more like a natural spring than a man-made object. Lights dotted around revealed a jacuzzi that fed into the pool, as well as a number of beach chairs and what looked like a swim-up bar. A staircase on the far side of the porch led down to the lagoon area, which boasted numerous palm trees, spiky shrubs, and other tropical flowers and plants.

There were quite a few people down by the pool, enjoying it as if it were the middle of the afternoon. I guess for the vampires, it pretty much was. Women with skimpy bikinis and men without their shirts were being waited on by servers dressed in black and white. As high as we were, I could hear the splashing water below. But my eyes were drawn to the man sitting in an alcove nearby on an overstuffed couch, being fanned from behind by two gorgeous female vampires, each of whom holding a wide palm frond.

"Ah, Cassandra," said Varycas, opening his arms wide. "How good it is to see you again. I was hoping that you might stop by to see me sometime." No sign of Jacquelyn. Where was she? Had she not anticipated me bringing my complaint to the highest vampire authority in the area? "And Mill, it is good to see you as well. Things are still going well for your star-crossed romance?"

Mill inclined his head in a sort of bow that was so noncommittal that it made me wince.

"Well, now, why don't you all join me? We can sit and catch up. How does that sound?"

A trickle of fear moved down my spine as I stared at the sofa across from Varycas. Out of the corner of my eye, I saw his chief servant standing by, just beneath a cover of shadow.

Was I really about to do this again? Was this going to be

my life for the rest of forever? Dragging myself to the Lord of Tampa, begging for his help, always at his mercy?

This didn't seem right. This was going to have to stop.

But Jacquelyn needed to be stopped.

And this was my only way forward.

With halting steps, I settled myself on the seat before him and readied myself to speak.

31

"There now, isn't that better?" Varycas asked, leaning back against his own sofa, his arms spread out over the back of it as if he meant to bask in the sunshine.

We sat down on the couch, all three of us like little ducks in a row. The couch itself was definitely outdoor furniture, uncomfortable and stiff, made from that stretchy plastic material that never actually gets wet. I could feel the sweat beading up on the back of my legs as we sat there.

"There is nothing better than living in Florida, I can tell you that from long experience. I spent several centuries in my dear old England...and she served me well. But I was ready for a bit of warmth, you see. Ready to expand my horizons. See what it was like to live somewhere entirely new." He gave me a sidelong look, smiling broadly at me. "I hear that you and your family did something very similar. Moved from the snowy north to our sun-drenched shores. How have you enjoyed living here, Cassandra?"

My knee jerk reaction was to correct him, just like I corrected everyone else...but realized quickly enough just how stupid that would really be.

Mill stiffened beside me. We were all sitting so closely together on the couch that our arms were all pressed against one another, while Varycas sprawled across his own couch, smiling at us across the divide.

Yeah, it probably wouldn't really be that smart for me to ignore his question, as much as I didn't want his attention on me or my life.

More than that, why did he care? I get that he was into small talk and whatnot, but like...why was he as weirdly interested in me as Draven was? What was it about *me* that drew the attention of vampires?

"I love it here," I said, sitting casually back against the sofa, crossing one leg over the other. "Even as hot as it is. I was never all that happy back in New York. I didn't really leave all that much behind."

"So I've heard," he said. He smiled, his voice trailing off, as if he was lost in thought.

He had, huh? Just how close had he and Jacquelyn become?

"Would you all like something to drink?" he asked. "It is rather humid out this evening, isn't it? Especially for you red-blooded folk."

I glanced at Mill, who was watching me closely. It was obvious he was not comfortable with this. He hadn't been the last time we met with Varycas, but what did we have to be afraid of now?

"Why don't you go whip something up for us?" Varycas said, looking over his shoulder and smiling at his chief servant. The servant bowed deeply to Varycas and started toward the doors. An aura of darkness clung to him like I always imagined vampires to have. There would be no mistaking him for a human. He looked too...predatory. Too much like a jungle cat, or a snake.

"There now," Varycas said, settling back into the sofa. He looked over at Mill. "I hope that things are treating you well, Mill."

Mill inclined his head. "Yes, Lord Varycas. As good as they can be." He gave me a glance, and a shiver ran down my spine. Nice, Mill. Why don't you just tell him that I'm pissed at you? And then you can tell him why.

"Good, good," Varycas said, nodding his head.

"It looks as if you are settling into the role of Lord of Tampa," Xandra said.

I winced. I hadn't explained to Xandra that she basically was nothing more than a servant for Mill. He was technically the one in charge while we were here.

Varycas turned his eyes to her for the first time since we had sat down. "Indeed I am," he said, and I could have sworn I saw a dangerous flash in his eyes. "This is what an informal night looks like around here. What peace looks like." He chuckled. "I must admit, I am rather fond of evenings like this." He waved a hand down at the crowd below. "What about you? How have your evenings been now that peace has fallen over Tampa?"

"Oh, well..." I said. "It's been all right, until this evening. But tonight was kind of a rough one, honestly."

There was a sharp jab to my ribs from Mill. Why wouldn't I tell him what was happening? Wasn't that the whole reason why we were here? Or did he not appreciate the informal language I was using with Varycas?

Varycas's expression changed. Cool nonchalance became curiosity. "Why? What happened?" he said, folding his hands in his lap.

I let out a breath that I hadn't realized I had been holding. He was still on our side, after all. That made it all that much better. Maybe he would be able to get Jacquelyn out of here. Or at least keep her away from me.

"We were attacked," I said. "By vampires. In downtown Tampa outside of a theater."

"Vampires?" Varycas nodded his head. "That must have been rather terrifying."

"It was," I said.

The door leading out onto the porch swung open, and the chief servant reappeared, a silver tray in his hands.

"Ah, good, I was hoping you were on your way," Varycas said.

The chief servant set the tray down on the coffee table in front of us, the china clinking ever so softly as he did.

There were four teacups and saucers, all with the same blue and white floral pattern. The dark liquid inside the cups were steaming. A metallic tang filled the air, and my stomach clenched. The chief servant passed the first teacup to Varycas.

"Thank you, Alfred," he said with a sigh. He brought the teacup closer to him, inhaling deeply. "Wonderful. You'll have to tell me what you think of this blend."

Alfred passed the next cup to Mill, who sniffed his cup cautiously.

I watched Alfred lift the last two teacups and saucers warily. They were steaming, just like Varycas's and Mill's... but he wouldn't be so insane, would he? It was dark on the porch, even with the flickering tiki torches and chandelier overhead. The liquid was dark. That was just black tea, right? I didn't really like black tea at all, unless it was ice cold and filled with sugar. Still, I took the cup from Alfred, whose eyebrows must have been permanently furrowed.

The cup was warm in my fingers, almost too hot to hold. The china looked ancient, making me all the more nervous about holding it. I didn't think he would be all that happy with me if I were to let it slip out of my hand and shatter on the ground. The liquid inside was dark and thick, leaving red streaks up the side of the cup. The movement of the liquid released its scent into the air...and my stomach turned over.

It was blood. Varycas was serving us blood. I swallowed hard, trying to move the cup as far from my nose as possible, as discreetly as possible.

Varycas was happily sipping on his own teacup, smiling as if there was nothing wrong in the world. Movement beside me drew my eyes, and I watched as Mill lifted the teacup to his own lips. Slowly, he took a sip from the delicate cup.

My stomach turned over, and I wanted to get up and run away. As he lowered the cup, I watched his tongue lick the rest of the deep red blood from his lips, and my mind was swarmed with memories of his hulking form bending over the body of that man...

I looked away, disgusted.

"That hits the spot," Varycas said, smacking his lips. I did my very best to keep my eyes on his, and not the half-drained cup in his hands. It was taking all of my strength to keep my hands from shaking and therefore rattling the cup against the saucer.

"My apologies, Cassandra, you were telling me about your evening?" Varycas asked.

It was hard to think with the smell of blood so strong in my nose.

"We were wondering if there was something that you could do to make sure something like this doesn't happen again," I said. "I realize that you warned me there would be deaths, but...right out in the open? People were killed tonight, others seriously injured. It just seems antithetical to the peace that we'd talked about before."

"Are you asking for my protection?" Varycas asked, cocking his head at me.

"Not exactly, no," I said. "But you want to keep the peace as much as I do, right?"

He nodded his head. "Indeed I do."

"Then you have to do something about Jacquelyn," I said.

"What does Jacquelyn have to do with it?"

"She was there," I said. "She was the one who ordered the attack."

An amused expression passed over his face, his eyes narrowing. "Jacquelyn?" he said. He shook his head. "No...no, indeed not." And then his eyes gleamed with amusement. "I was the one who ordered that attack."

32

I didn't even have time to blink before I was thrown against one of the pillars supporting the structure of the porch. Hands with the strength of an iron grip clenched tightly around my throat. Stars appeared in my eyes as I struggled to draw a breath. My feet were kicked out from beneath me, and I realized with horror that I was hovering above the ground, held up only by the hands around my neck. I struggled to pull my gaze into focus.

Mill was in the background, scuffling with Varycas. The sofa had tipped over backwards, and with snarling like wild animals, they were attempting to outmaneuver the other.

I looked down and realized that it was Alfred holding me against the pillar, a wide, wicked grin splitting his face. I grasped at his hands, desperately trying to pry them away. My strength was quickly fading as my brain was depraved of the oxygen I needed. There was a cry of pain, and I slammed into the ground.

"Come on," Xandra's voice said. Another hand gripped my wrist, warm this time, and dragged me to my feet.

"What happened?" I asked, rubbing my throat as we hurried away from the pillar.

"I stabbed him," she said, looking around wildly for somewhere to go. "Right in the elbow. It seemed to work, at least for now."

"Thanks," I said.

"Don't thank me yet," she said. "We've still gotta figure out how we're getting out of this nest of hornets."

"Hornets only sting you," I said. We were blocked in. The vampires down by the pool had heard the commotion up on the porch, and many of them were hurrying up the sprawling staircases. "I think these guys intend to do much worse." The doors slammed open, and guards like the ones at the entrance to the estate were there, looking around wildly.

Crap. They were literally everywhere. It was like the street outside of the theater all over again. There was no way we were going to be able to fight our way out of this.

"Uh...Cass?" Xandra said. We had maneuvered to stand back to back, watching as vampires began to circle around us from every side, blocking our exit toward the pool or the doors. We were trapped.

"Yeah?" I said.

"Please tell me that you have an idea. Or at the very least, a stake somewhere?"

Like one stake was going to do anything. I nailed my shin against something hard, sending a sharp pain up my leg. I looked down and saw a small, wooden side table. The legs were narrow and interwoven with wicker. It wasn't much, but it would have to do.

"Cover your head," I told Xandra, and picked up the small table, then slammed it onto the concrete patio. The table legs splintered and broke off. Which was exactly what

I was hoping they would do. "Here," I said, wiping my sweaty hair from my eyes. "Take this–"

But Alfred had returned, Xandra's stake still sticking out of his elbow. Blood trickled down his arm like black spider-webs, the droplets clinging to the tips of his fingers. It didn't seem to bother him much, though. He flexed his fingers and rolled his shoulders. He lunged at Xandra and me, and we leapt away from each other just in time. He adjusted, turning to leap at me, but I was ready with the broken table leg held out in front of myself like a samurai holding a katana. This was how I had killed Byron, after all.

Alfred slammed into the table leg...but all it did was splinter and break in half. He snickered as he yanked the remnants of it out of my hand. He wore a nasty leer, the perfect expression for him.

One second he was there, the next he was on the floor, with someone struggling, pinning him to the ground. Mill looked up with bared teeth; he had another gash across the side of his face, and the sleeve of his shirt was torn. "Run," he said, before pulling Alfred's arms behind his back to restrain him.

"Come on," Xandra said.

The other guards tried to charge at us, but Mill somehow managed to be the tank he always was and jumped in between them and us.

Xandra stopped just before the edge of the balcony, staring over the banister. "We have to jump," she said, staring down onto the driveway.

"That's a full story drop," I said.

"Not if we land on the car," she said.

A very nice candy apple red Lamborghini sat just below us.

"That's insane," I said. "We'll break our legs."

"We'll be fine," she said. "Besides, do you really want to stay here and let them finish what Jacquelyn started?"

"I hate that you're right," I said. Before I could even stop her, she hopped over the railing, and disappeared from sight. "Xandra!"

She landed deftly on the top of the car, the metal crunching beneath her weight. She turned and looked up at me. "Come on, you'll be fine." In the distance, I could see shapes moving in the shadows of the lawn. We had to get out now, or we were going to get stuck.

As I launched myself over the side, a familiar, gut wrenching sensation coursed through me, as if I had left my stomach back up on the balcony. That moment of being suspended in the air with no guarantee that I would land safely might be exhilarating for some people. For me, it was just terrifying.

I struck the top of the car, and my training with Mill kicked in before I even had time to think about it. I bent my legs in order to absorb the shock of the impact. The top of the car, which had already been dented from Xandra's jump crumpled even more beneath my weight. I tried not to take it personally.

Xandra was already on the ground, her body poised to run around the side of the house back toward the limo. I had no idea what we were going to do when we got there, but at least we would be that much closer to escaping. My heart filled with dread. What were we going to do even if we managed to escape?

"Let's go." Xandra dashed around the corner of the house, her arms pumping, purple hair flowing out behind her like the mane of a unicorn. So far, the guards hadn't caught us. Were they more concerned about protecting

Varycas than catching up with us? Or had Mill somehow managed to distract them enough?

I heard Xandra shriek before I made my way around the corner, making my heart stop for a second. I pushed myself even farther, even faster, forcing my panic down so it didn't bubble up and completely overwhelm me. I turned the corner at a sprint, and found–

Alfred had her. He was holding her in a joint lock, the black blood still oozing from his arm. She was fighting, trying as hard as she could to get away, to pull her arms free. He twisted, and she let out a short scream.

The limo was still parked in front of the house a short distance away. Guards were starting to swarm closer. With horror, I realized that some of them were not vampires at all. They were humans, running toward us with flashlights in their hands, their movements far less graceful and slower. Varycas had humans working for him?

The closest guard's skin looked almost papery, his eyes sunken and dark. It was almost as if he wasn't all there. Were the vampires using him to feed? That was the only thing I could think of that would explain his horrifying appearance.

Suddenly, Mill was there, sliding in front of me like Michael Jackson in "Thriller" at the same time that one of the human guards was charging at me. Mill didn't even hesitate. He grabbed the guard's head in his hands. I was immediately grateful that I had the sense to look away, because there was a sickening *crack* as Mill snapped his neck.

"Mill!" I cried. "What the...?"

"He was going to kill you," Mill said.

"That was a human," I said, horrified.

"Cassie!" Xandra shouted; Alfred was dragging her toward the doors.

"We have to get her," I said.

Mill caught my arm as I stared forward. "We're about to have more company."

I whipped around and saw Varycas hurrying toward us with some of the vamps dressed in their swimsuits. Behind them were even more guards, and with a sinking feeling in my stomach, I saw still more guards appearing through the front doors. Just how many of them were there?

"We're leaving," Mill said.

"Get Xandra," I said.

But he ignored me. He wrapped his arms around me, tossed me over his shoulder, and started running. The ground blurred beneath him, concrete drive giving way to dark grass that rippled like waves on the ocean. I went along, stunned for a few seconds, until I heard Xandra's cry from the doorway.

Then I struggled in Mill's arms, trying to break free, to tumble back down to the ground, but Mill held me tightly against his shoulder. "Don't do this," I yelled. "Don't you dare leave without her–"

He didn't reply. He just ran, the world blurring into darkness as we left the lights of the house farther and farther behind. Palm trees and other tropical plants blocked my view as we disappeared into a planter and, a moment later, he leapt the wall surrounding the estate. We landed, hard, a moment later, pain shooting through my stomach as I caught Mill's shoulder in a landing that made my leap onto the Lamborghini seem like a gentle step down by comparison.

My stomach, already writhing in pain from that, dropped as the realization of what we'd just done settled over me.

We had left Xandra behind.
I had abandoned her.

33

X andra. How could I have let her get kidnapped? How had this happened to her so many times? I was there this time, I could have stopped it.

Mill could have stopped it.

"I can't believe you just...left her," I said.

My voice was hollow, quiet. I didn't even have the strength to scream, even though my heart was shattering into a thousand pieces. I couldn't move. My body was frozen, paralyzed with fear.

Xandra was in danger. And it was entirely my fault.

"It was either save her or you," he said. He had transferred me to his back, carrying me piggyback now. Not that I was actually doing anything to hold on. My arms were around his neck, but his arms were the ones supporting my legs. "And I'm sorry, but given that choice, I am always going to save you."

I had no idea how far we had gone from the mansion, or how Mill had managed to lose the other vampires following after us. The sounds of the city surrounded us; cars were driving by, their lights flashing in my eyes. The cicadas screeched in the darkness, hidden from sight. A dog barked in someone's backyard.

I didn't know what time it was. I didn't know where we were.

"She's my best friend, Mill, and I just...I left her behind."

I was suddenly reminded of when I watched Jacquelyn get kidnapped back in New York. History repeats itself.

Why did this keep happening to me?

"Where are we going?" I asked.

"Back to the Lockwood's," he said.

"Fine," I said.

It was not fine.

"Do you mind if I run again for a while?" Mill asked.

"Do whatever you want," I said. Right up there with 'fine' in terms of lies I told these days.

He started to pick up the pace.

"Because you do whatever you want anyways, don't you?"

His footsteps slowed.

"What do you mean by that?" he asked.

"Just that," I said. "It doesn't matter what I think, or what I want. You do whatever you want without even thinking about the consequences of your actions."

"I already told you, I didn't want to leave Xandra, but I had to. If I had left you even for a second, Varycas would have come at you. And since he was the one who ordered the attack, then he is the one who wants you dead. He probably could not care less about Xandra, aside from using her to get to you."

"That's not the only thing I am talking about," I said. The anger was swelling inside of me like a water balloon, heating my insides, my blood starting to boil. "You killed that man just now. The guard. As if he were nothing more

than an animal. And that man outside of the restaurant...
Mill, you killed him, too."

Mill was quiet for a while, so long that I wondered if he
had heard me at all in the first place. I was just about to
open my mouth and yell at him when he finally replied. "I
did all of those things to protect you."

"That's not a good enough reason," I snapped. "You
could have always made another choice. You could have
disabled that guard, and you could have just left that guy at
the restaurant."

"Cassie, you don't understand. He was going to die
anyway. Those vampires had done a number on him.
Crushed his ribs, broken both of his arms. His internal
bleeding was irreparable." All I could see was the top of his
head, and I wanted to pound on it like a bongo drum. He
sounded so cold, so uncaring. My stomach turned at the
thought of that poor man, lying there dying on the street.

"And you think that you were being merciful by draining
him?" I said.

Mill exhaled quickly. "You really don't understand.
When vampires drain a human, it doesn't cause them any
pain. If anything, it just knocks them out, and–"

"That's disgusting," I said. "I don't want to hear the intri-
cacies of how you kill your victims."

"I did it to heal myself. So I could protect you."

"Yeah, well, Iona was protecting me, too, and I didn't see
her stooping to drink some easy blood," I said.

"Iona was the one who had to get carried to the car,
didn't she?" Mill asked.

"That doesn't make it okay, Mill," I said.

"So you would have preferred that I fell to Jacquelyn's
assailants, let you and all of your friends get captured, and
be turned into slaves or vampires?"

I was quiet for a few moments. Of course that wasn't what I wanted.

"There was no other choice," Mill said. "And I don't regret what I did."

He picked up his pace again, now that the street was clear of cars. We ran past the dark houses along the side of the street. In the distance, I could see the glow from Tampa's bright city lights mingling with the clouds overhead.

"You're a monster," I whispered.

Mill did not answer. He just kept running.

34

We got back to Lockwood's just as the first hints of dawn filled the air. Birds had started to call to each other, sprinkler systems were kicking on before the heat of the sun could leach the moisture from the earth, and the morning commuters were pulling up to Starbucks or Dunkin', their lines stretching all the way around the buildings.

Lockwood's house was as unassuming as all of the others on the street. Newspapers were already sitting on people's front porches, and only a few homes had lights on in their windows. Mill slowed to a stop in front of Lockwood's sidewalk, where he let me down off his back. My legs were stiff, all of the blood rushing back to the sleeping vessels. I staggered for a second, grabbing onto him for support. We glanced at each other, and I pushed away from him, staggering back toward the door.

I knocked, and Lockwood answered after the second rap of my knuckles on the blue door. "You're back," he said. He peered over my shoulder at the empty driveway. "...without the limo?"

"Xandra's been kidnapped," I said.

"What?" It was Laura who asked; she stood right behind Lockwood.

When I looked at her, my heart breaking all over again, her eyes widened and her cheeks drained of color. "It wasn't Jacquelyn who ordered the attack on us at the theater," I said. "It was Varycas."

"That is...unfortunate," Lockwood said. He ushered us inside.

"You're all scratched up," Laura said. "Let me wake up your dad–"

"No, it's fine," I said. "I really don't want to have to tell them...everything. Besides, we have to come up with a plan to break her out."

"Break who out?" This was Iona. She was up on her feet, and wearing clean clothes. All things considered, she looked good as new. Her eyes widened as she took in the two of us. "They got Xandra? How?"

"The whole place was swarming," Mill said.

"I thought that much would be obvious," Iona said.

"Varycas turned on us," Mill said. "I'd say it came out of nowhere, but..." He shook his head.

"He did what?" Gregory asked. He and Derrick had just walked into the room. Gregory's hair was all messed up as if he had fallen asleep on an arm of the couch. Derrick's eyes were bloodshot and he was squinting, the light too strong for him.

"We were sitting there just talking with him," I said, "when he started going on about how great his life was at his swanky mansion. Tried to act like the nice guy, offering us drinks...which was blood by the way."

"Ew, gross," Laura said, shuddering.

"In teacups. Though some among us didn't seem to care..." I said, flicking a glare in Mill's direction.

Laura's eyes narrowed in disgust as she looked up at Mill.

"I was being polite," Mill said. "I had no idea that he would give you blood as well."

"Quite the message," Lockwood said. "Rather bold, don't you think?"

"Disturbing, more like," Derrick said, his nose wrinkling.

"How did the fight start?" Iona asked. I could tell she was irritated.

"He was asking what I wanted him to do," I said, "and I told him that he needed to do something about Jacquelyn. He got this weird, creepy look on his face and was all like, 'Jacquelyn? Oh, no...I was the one who ordered that attack.'"

"He ordered it?" Laura asked, her mouth gaping.

"But why?" Derrick said. "What about the peace?"

"That slimy, pretentious, power-hungry–" Lockwood said.

Iona folded her arms. "I for one, am not surprised."

"What do you mean?" I asked.

"You don't realize how much of a threat you are, do you?" Iona said. "Draven's minions called you a slayer, didn't they? It isn't hard to imagine that he wanted to get you out of the picture so you didn't turn on him like you did on Draven."

"I didn't turn on Draven," I said. "I was defending myself every step of the way."

Iona shrugged her shoulders. "Doesn't matter. You have killed vampires. And not just one, and not on accident. Try to go back to the cattle analogy–"

"I'm not easily offended," I said, "but if you keep calling me a cow I'm gonna eventually get there."

"–because if there was a cow that killed a human," Iona went on, "you could maybe chalk it up to an accident. If a cow massacred a whole office complex of humans–"

"According to Troy McClure, they would if they could," Gregory said under his breath.

"–then suddenly you're dealing with something very different," Iona said. "Especially if the cow continues to evade all efforts at being put down."

I tried not to roll my eyes too hard at that. "And yet, these vamps still manage to keep kidnapping my friends and my family." I hesitated, thinking it over. "He really thinks I'm a dire threat?"

"As new Lord of Tampa, he isn't going to leave anyone hanging around that can interfere with his authority," Iona said. "Part of getting hold of power is eliminating rivals for it, and you killed his predecessor. If he really means to take you out of the picture, though, he is going to use Xandra as leverage."

My heart fluttered hopefully. "You think so?"

"What would be the point in killing her?" Iona said. "All it would do is piss you off, and he has heard stories about you when you were pissed off. He isn't going to want to deal with that. Expect a hostage exchange."

"It sounds to me as if Varycas is more intelligent than his predecessor," Lockwood said. "He isn't going to underestimate you or your willingness to fight. Using Xandra as a hostage to manipulate you into doing what he wants? A much more sound strategy."

"They are going to use her as bait to draw us back?" Laura said. "Isn't that what Draven did, too?"

Mill's jaw was clenched, and he was staring at the floor,

the leaves of the forest floor that Lockwood had created for his home trapped beneath his feet. "Yes. And it'd be foolish to chomp at the bait."

I glared at him, and he didn't say anything else. "I walked out of Draven's alive, didn't I?"

"Draven didn't have hurricane shutters," he said.

"Lockwood is right," Iona said. "Varycas knows what you did to Draven and all of his cronies. You think that you can go in with the same battle plan, but that isn't going to work."

"Not only that, but you have an enemy that knows you quite well," Lockwood said.

"What, you mean Jacquelyn?" I said. I snorted with derision. "Yeah, no. She doesn't know me, not anymore. She knew the New York me. Pre-vampire me. I am not the same person I was when I burned Jacquelyn."

"You can do this," Laura said. Her eyes were shining with pride. "You've done it before. How many vampires have you killed?"

Mill fidgeted, his jaw working. I could see the tightness near his eyes. He was dying to say something, but Iona stepped in before he did.

"It doesn't matter," she said. "You could have killed one or one thousand. Varycas is a different beast. Even if you don't think Jacquelyn knows you, she knows you enough to understand who and what is important to you, and she has such a grudge against you that she makes the perfect attack dog."

I chewed on my lip. "So you don't think I should go?"

Iona blinked at me. "Of course you shouldn't, are you stupid?"

"Then who's going to get Xandra back?" I said. "This wouldn't have happened if someone helped me to get her while we were still there."

Mill winced as if I had struck him physically, but the anger was simmering just beneath the surface. I could see it in the tension of his shoulders, the pursing of his lips. Maybe it wasn't fair that I was attacking him in front of everyone else, but I had a lot of emotions coursing through me, and a big part of me really didn't care how he felt about anything right then.

"I am not going to leave her there," I said. "I refuse."

Worry creased Lockwood's forehead, and he scratched his chin. His bright green eyes were fixated on me as if I were some strange specimen he was observing. "I admire your dedication to your friends, Cassandra...but even you must see how dangerous this is."

"I'm not saying it's not dangerous," I said. "I was there when Varycas's minions went off on us, I know how dangerous it is. But she would come back for me, too, no matter what. And I would never forgive myself if anything happened to her."

Gregory nodding his head. "Yeah. We can't leave Xandra behind...even if she does call me a little boy."

Iona sighed, shaking her head. "Your parents are not going to be happy with this...again."

"Yeah, well, that's kind of normal now, isn't it?"

Iona pinched the bridge of her nose. "This is not the first time that she's been a hostage. Does this girl ever not get captured?"

"If I have anything to do with it, this is the last time," I said. "And if we're lucky and he's smart, it'll teach Varycas not to mess with me anymore."

"Are you talking about trying to take Varycas out?" Iona asked in disbelief. "You cannot be serious."

"No," I said. "But I do want to teach him to leave me alone. If he leaves me alone, I leave him alone. I told him this already, and he seems to think that I wasn't serious. Well...he's going to learn just how serious I was."

"Bold talk," Mill said. "But that's all it is unless you've got a plan to back it up."

"I'm working on one," I said. "Anyone who wants in, let me know."

"Count me in," Gregory said.

"Yeah, me too," Laura said.

"This sounds thoroughly insane." Iona just shook her head. "Of course that means I'm in."

A hard grip on my upper arm stopped the recitation cold. Mill was there, face stone-like, eyes blazing. "I need to talk to you. Alone." And he let go of me, stalking off behind a pair of tall trees.

"Go," Lockwood said, watching me with kind, if slightly worried eyes. "I am with you in this. And when you return, I may have something that will...help. Somewhat."

"Thank you, Lockwood," I said, gracing him with a small smile. It was all I could manage at the moment. He bowed, and I nodded to him, then followed the path that Mill had taken through this odd forest that was Lockwood's home.

35

I found Mill only a few steps behind the trees, but probably a room away from where I'd left the others. He was beside a brook that babbled its way through. Mossy rocks sat in the riverbed, providing a little green against the brown stones. Mill was pacing back and forth next to the rushing waters, a distracted look on his face, his high brow furrowed.

"What do you want?" I asked, a little coldly, even to my ears. I was in no mood.

"I can't believe you're thinking about attacking Varycas's estate," Mill said. His agitation was obvious. "We barely made it out alive last time."

"Yes, *we* did," I said. "You and me. This time, we'll have help."

"Your help is less than helpful," Mill said, turning mid-pace like a bull stomping his hoof. "Iona's not at a hundred percent. Lockwood is the best fighter you've got, but he can only do so much. These are some long odds you're playing."

"You're forgetting my other friends," I said. "They–"

"Are humans, and less than useless in this fight," Mill

said, his voice like gravel. "You've been in enough scrapes with vampires to understand: even with training, you people are treading water in a fight with us, at best. This is suicide for you."

I tried to hold my head high against his verbal assault. "Well, I just don't see it that way."

Mill clenched a fist and turned his head away. "That's the whole problem you're having right now, Cassie."

"Um, my problem is vampires," I said, keeping mine on him. "Of all varieties."

He looked back over his shoulder. "You really don't get it, do you? The reason you're looking at me the way you are right now is the way you should have seen me – us – all along."

"As a monster?" I asked, my voice feeling brittle and crystalline.

"Yes," he said, looking at me with those dark eyes. "You've seen the monstrous side of me because I'm dealing with monsters. Because I'm trying to protect you from them."

"You can't protect me without becoming one of them?"

He shook his head slowly. "You're living in a fantasy world, Cassie. A lie, if you will. You think that you can be decent or human or unwilling to make the tough, atrocious choices I've made and still survive this. You can't. You just want to live your life, but they want to eat you. It's a different in attitude, in viciousness. You're a child walking along a beach with no chaperone and they're the sharks three feet out in the surf. You don't know what you're walking into when you play in the waves, and you won't listen to me." Now he was growling.

"Why don't you look yourself in the mirror and ask why I might not trust or listen to you right now?" I asked coldly.

Mill cocked his head. "Because...I can't. I have no reflection."

"Oh." I felt oddly frozen in place, embarrassed by my lack of foresight in that answer. "Well...you look a lot more monstrous lately. Guess you'll have to take my word for it." I kept my distance. "I saw you drink a random stranger, Mill."

"I did it to protect–"

"I don't care why you did it," I said. "I saw what I saw. I saw you become a monster to supposedly protect me from the monsters. Except we fought them before and never had to get that...dirty."

"When you fought them before, they weren't ready for you," Mill said. "They were arrogant and unprepared. Now you're the one who's arrogant, thinking that you can just walk into this world and bowl over any vamp that gets in your way. But you can't, Cassie. You've survived because of luck and skill, but not in equal measure, and your luck's run out." He shook his head slowly. "You need to walk away from this while you can. Take your friends, take your family...and just go. Get out of this territory. Don't challenge Varycas in his home court. Just...run."

"Something you should have figured out about me by now," I said, tracing a path away from him. "I'm not much of a runner. It's why I hate PE class, and never got into track."

"Cassie," he called after me, right before I rounded the trunk. "Please. If not for me...for your friends."

I turned and gave him one last look. "I am thinking about my friends. And the one you left behind." His face fell as I rounded the trunk, leaving him by the edge of the stream, and he knew he'd failed to sway me.

36

My parents were sleeping in a little glen off the main entry to the house. It reminded me of the room I had been given when staying at the castle of the Seelie, more a meadow than a bedroom. Trees made up the bed posts and the canopy above was bright, green leaves. Moonlight gleamed through the branches, the perfect nightlight.

Dad was snoring softly on his back. Mom was curled in a ball, snuggling up to the oversized pillow in her arms. I stood off to the side, watching them, a strange reversal of how they'd probably been when I was a baby. I really hated the idea of waking them, wondering if I should just leave without saying anything. There was zero chance I wanted to bring either of them with me. Unlike my friends, they'd never really rumbled with vampires before. Still, if anything were to happen, I needed them to know where I was and what had happened.

Climbing over the bottom of the bed, I mimicked the action of my childhood and wormed my way up between them. It didn't take much effort; the bed was massive, and there was plenty of room in the middle. Mom roused as I snuggled in, inhaling deeply as she stretched her arm out across my body. "Mmm, hi, sweetie," she said. "How did the meeting go?" Like she was asking me about a scholarship interview or something, like a normal teen.

Dad started moving when he heard Mom's voice. "Cassie?" his voice was bleary with sleep.

"Hey Mom, Dad," I said. I slipped beneath the sheets. The bed was nice and warm, and not because either of them had been sleeping on this part. It seemed to be just naturally so, another little splash of Fae magic sprinkled in. "It went...um...not well." Their eyes found me in the dark. "Xandra kinda...snuck into the car with us and...she got left behind."

"Oh, no," my mother said softly.

"So...I have to go back," I said. "Varycas is going to do the whole 'hostage, bait' thing to get me back, I'm sure, but...I can't just leave her behind."

Mom rubbed my arm affectionately, a tight smile on her lips. "Of course you can't."

I blinked. "Uh...you're taking this surprisingly well."

"Well," she said, "over the last few months, I've seen that you aren't the little girl that I used to push on the swings anymore. You've grown into a young woman who is capable of making her own decisions, and able to see the consequences of those decisions. For a long time, I thought you were just selfish and immature, the way you were lying about everything. But all of this nonsense with the vampires...it's changed you. And I do think, as hard as it has been...it has changed you for the better."

"Oh," I said, unsure of how to take that.

"Doesn't mean I'm happy about you walking into the hornet's nest again," she said. "Just...please, stay safe. We have been through too much to lose you now."

"I know, Mom," I said. "I was really hoping this was the end of it."

"Is there no way to avoid this?" Dad asked. "Couldn't the vampires just go for you? They are more equipped to handle this sort of thing."

"No, Dad, I have to go. Varycas wants me, after all. And if I don't go, I'm afraid they'll hurt Xandra. I can't let them do that to her, not because I might be afraid."

Dad swallowed nervously, looking away. "That's what I figured. But you're just a kid, Cassie. A kid who has had to see more in her life already than most ever see in their whole lives. It just...isn't fair."

My heart clenched. Dad was never so disheartened. He was genuinely fearful about all of this. It wasn't like him to let his emotions govern his thoughts like this. It was making me sick to my stomach. If *he* was worried, then what was I getting myself into?

"All that matters is that I get Xandra out," I said. "After that, we can deal with what comes next. I think Lockwood's place is safe."

"You don't want us to come with you?" Dad asked.

I shook my head. "No. I need you two to be safe. I wouldn't be able to focus if you were in harm's way. And unfortunately, the odds are good that we will be coming back with wounded, in which case I'll need your help getting them all patched back up."

His face paled. "Okay."

"Promise you'll be safe?" Mom asked. "And that you will listen to Iona and Mill if they tell you it's too dangerous?"

"If I did, I'd be lying, Mom," I said. She didn't like that answer, but she did accept it with a curt, pained nod.

"Just make sure you come back," Dad said. "In one piece, all right?"

"I will," I said.

Mom opened her arms and I leaned in to embrace her, Dad wrapping his arms around the both of us. I felt like a child again, for one blissful moment. Like I was a kid in bed with Mom and Dad on a Saturday morning, no worries about vampires and monsters and all else.

But at least I knew they would be safe. One less thing for me to worry about.

"Hey, you okay?" Laura was the first to hurry over to me as I stepped back into the main living space, that forested space where we came in the front door. She sat with the others in the shade of tall trees, a slow breeze whispering through.

"I'm fine," I said. "Just...dealing with everything."

She put a hand on my shoulder. "You know, I've been thinking about what you said, and I think you are totally right. Xandra wouldn't have hesitated to come back for us."

I smiled at her. "You're right, Laura. And I appreciate you pointing it out. It's easy to get caught up in the fact that this is a crazy thing we're doing, rather than remembering that as crazy as it is, Xandra would do the same for any of us."

"Not for just any of us." Iona said. She was standing with Lockwood, and they'd been talking in hushed voices. She raised hers now, though. "Cassie, we've been talking–"

I held up my hand. "Save it. You aren't talking me out of this, not now."

"Not what I was going to say," she said. "Lockwood has

something we could use, but it's going to require some tweaking."

"You don't want to talk me out of it?" I asked.

"If I wanted to waste my time, I'd rewatch *Game of Thrones*," she said. Then she sighed, shaking her head. "I'm always saving you, anyways, aren't I? Might as well save purple hair girl, too."

I grinned. "Thank you, Iona."

"And don't think I don't want a stab at Jacquelyn again," she said, arching an eyebrow at me. "She's been nothing but trouble."

The anger in me flared up again. "You aren't kidding."

"So, what's next?" Gregory asked, stepping up to the group. Derrick had been next to him, but had seemed to consciously hang back when Gregory came forward. From the distant look in his eyes, he seemed deep in thought. Somehow, I didn't think he'd tell me if I asked him. Was all of this reminding him of the chaos we went through with his dad? Ever since the vamps showed up, he had been...off. I was worried, but didn't have enough energy to worry about him right now, too. I tried to make eye contact, but he didn't even seem to notice me.

"Preparations are underway," Lockwood said.

"Are you guys coming or not?" I asked them.

Gregory looked over his shoulder at Derrick, who finally lifted his head.

"Oh, I'm in," Gregory said. "Been working on my Call of Duty skills, ready to engage in both close and ranged combat."

I snorted. "I'm sure that'll be incredibly helpful."

"I'm serious," he said. "You gotta admit it was awesome when I vaulted your fence that one night and started taking out vamps with holy water, right? And I wasn't a complete waste back on the street tonight. I didn't have a stake, but I didn't get hurt, either. Then the driving of the limo! See how valuable I am? You need me." He grinned.

"How can I possibly argue with all that evidence?" I asked. "Welcome aboard, and I hope you know what you're getting into."

"Low chance of success, high odds of death," Gregory said soberly. "Yeah. We all know."

I looked behind him at Derrick. "What about you? No judgment either way."

"Oh, we're judging," Gregory said. "I think you're crazy if you come with us."

Derrick looked up at me, and I could see regret in his gaze. "Yeah...I'm gonna pass," he said. "I wouldn't really be much help. I'd just end up as Xandra, part deux."

I wasn't sure I had ever heard that level of defeat in his voice. "You wouldn't end up like Xandra," I said. Where was all of this self-consciousness coming from? It was unlike him.

"I sure felt helpless tonight when the vampires swarmed us on the street. Please, I just..." He shook his head. "...I'll just stay here."

"I do understand, Derrick," I said. "But please know that you aren't worthless to any of us, okay?"

He gave me a weak smile. "Thanks, Cassie."

"What about Jed?" Iona asked.

"I tried calling him," I said, shrugging. "No answer at the store. Though I'm not surprised, given it's the middle of the night. And he doesn't have a cell phone, so..."

"Maybe we should get him one for emergencies," Laura suggested. "That way we could always have werewolf backup whenever we needed."

Lockwood seemed amused by this. "If we have gathered the troops, then I should like to show you the surprise that Iona mentioned." His eyes held a certain gleam to them. "Something that I think you will find will give us a significant leg up going into the belly of the beast."

38

S tanding on the street just down the road from the manor, my friends flanking me on both sides, waiting for dawn to come was one of the hardest waits of my life. This wasn't my first rodeo by any means, but that didn't mean these moments became any easier. If anything, it was harder to look down the quiet street and know that it wouldn't remain quiet for long. Blood would be spilled, and it was possible that I could lose one of my friends.

But those thoughts were paralyzing, and I had to shove them away.

Mill's motorcycle-helmeted head turned toward me, and through the blackened visor I could see...nothing. Iona, next to him, looked much the same though smaller and leaner. They watched me, waiting for my signal. Why, I had no idea. Why did it always have to be my decision?

The Florida heat was already present, even absent the sun. It was as if it radiated from the very sands, the concrete beneath my feet. I stared at Varycas's lush mansion, at the palm trees and tropical greenery that hemmed it in behind the perfect wall. Who knew what dangers lurked there?

Other than a host of vampires and a force of human guards, I didn't.

But Xandra...Xandra was in there somewhere.

There was no point waiting any longer.

"Let's go," I said.

Lockwood and Iona were off first, hurtling down the street toward the manor as surely as if I'd fired a starter pistol. They took the lead because I'd told them to, to keep Mill from getting out in front and dealing with the two human guards stationed out front. They were dressed in the same uniforms that I had seen the guys wearing last night.

Iona smashed into one, Lockwood blasted the other with a glint of magic I couldn't quite identify. They were both cleaned out instantly, and around we went, past the now-empty gate house and off the winding driveway.

More guards were there to meet us as we hurried across the lawn, the Saint Augustine sawgrass crunching beneath our boots and sneakers as we ran. They were all human, though, their faces exposed, their faces sallow like the others, the mark of a human sacrifice who'd been donating their blood to their master's cause.

Iona and Mill got in among them while Lockwood hung back with us humans; they dispatched them quickly, knocking them to the ground with skilled and precise force. I didn't see blood, or at least I didn't let my gaze linger too long to check. I had no desire to look too closely. I knew Iona would be merciful. Mill...

Well, that didn't bear thinking about.

The limo was still parked in the driveway where we left it, looking like it had been through a small war. The mansion's hurricane shutters were closed, keeping all of the vampires inside nice and protected from this ugly day.

Where was Xandra? Where would they be keeping her?

Probably with Varycas, no doubt. Did he know we were coming? Did we already trigger some sort of alarm? How did we know that there weren't going to be traps or tricks waiting for us inside?

Suddenly, this whole idea seemed crazy to me. In my blind desire to get Xandra back, had I completely overlooked the situation as a whole? Was I so obsessed with fixing my mistakes that I had led everyone into danger again? We hurried past the limo, the front door in sight. Mill was already there, lingering across from Iona, ready to kick it in.

Iona turned toward me, and she nodded.

I nodded back, readying my weapon, holding it up at the ready. Maybe they knew we were coming.

But they weren't going to expect *this*.

"Bring it on, baby," Gregory said, holding his weapon up, too.

Iona lashed out, kicking in the door. Mill shot past her, but she was in right after him, their motorcycle gear glinting in the sun. Light flooded into the darkened mansion, and with a deep breath, I charged, ready to be the first human into the fight.

39

W hen I hurried through the door to the mansion, the battle was already joined. Vampire guards were there in rows, already tangling with Mill and Iona. They were staying well back from the door, since the light of the sun was washing over the threshold.

My heart hammered against my chest, making it hard to think straight. The knowledge that Xandra was stuck somewhere inside this huge house was keeping me rooted to the spot. The blur of vampires moving and fighting made me pause in place in this sunlit segment of ground. Here, I was safe, at least for the moment.

I took a steadying breath and raised my hands, holding my crossbow up to my shoulder.

It was hard to follow the vampires' movements. The targets we had practiced on in Lockwood's magical dimension were stationary. I knew that it was just to get us comfortable with their weight, with the feel of pulling the trigger and absorbing the shock as the bolt was released. But the vampires that were fighting in front of us were moving so fast that they were almost a blur. I worried for the first time that I was going to hit Mill or Iona instead.

I steadied my hand as best as I could with a deep breath, looked down the sight, and pulled the trigger.

The bolt flew from the crossbow across the foyer...and shattered a porcelain vase.

"Crap," I said, lowering the crossbow, reloading a bolt.

Laura, who was standing right beside me, was standing there as if she had held a crossbow everyday of her life. She was completely still, her elbow held high just like Lockwood had taught her. I watched as she pulled the trigger, and less than a second later, a vampire across the room crumpled to the ground, the bolt buried in his chest.

"Holy cow, Laura," I said, holding my crossbow back up to my shoulder. "That was an amazing shot."

"Thanks," she said, jacking back the mechanism as she loaded another arrow. With a casual effort she brought it back up to her shoulder, then released another. Another vampire went down to gurking sounds, turning into goo.

Wow.

Mill and Iona had taken down a few themselves, fighting back to back like they were in some crazy martial arts movie. They were throwing punches and kicks faster than I could track, holding their own against the oncoming attackers.

Gregory almost passed me to run out of the sunbeam and into the house, but I snagged the back of his shirt. "Fire from the threshold." He was carrying a...slightly different weapon.

"Right," he said. "My whole life has been leading to this moment." He adjusted his glasses before holding his Super Soaker to his shoulder and drawing a bead. "You vampires are so screwed." He gave the gun one long pump before releasing a stream across four vamps that were circling up on Iona.

The holy water splashed against the exposed skin on the vampires' faces and hands. Unearthly shrieks echoed in the foyer. One vampire had gotten a whole face full of pain, skin slagging and melting off. He was howling in rage, blindly swinging his arms around in front of him, trying to make contact with Iona.

"Haha, suckers," Gregory said, releasing another torrent of water. I tried not to look too hard at what it did, given it melted skin in a hiss of steam, exposing bone and sinew and...ugh. Mill and Iona didn't slow their attack one bit, though, since they were covered from head to foot and were protected from the holy water splash. "You know, this is more Resident Evil with ammo and inventory management than it is DOOM." He gave his gun a good shake, checking the water levels in the bright blue tank.

There were shouts farther down the hall, and my heart skipped a beat as still more guards poured into the foyer. Was there no end to them? We had taken out almost a dozen already, and there seemed to be no shortage waiting to take their place. Laura released another bolt; the *twang* of the string rang in my right ear, the sound of the fighting echoed in my other.

I loosed another other bolt, away from Mill, easily over his shoulder. A scream resulted. I may not have been able to nail a heart shot like Laura, but I could at least do some damage, slow them down. The bolt hit a target, and my heart soared. And it was right in the heart, too.

But the body slumped against the ground, blood blooming out around from the wound like blotches of red paint.

My stomach sank. I had hit a human. I hadn't even realized that the humans had joined in the fighting in here.

What were they thinking? Did they care so little about
their own lives, their own well beings? Did they have no
families or friends? Why were they so ready to throw their
lives away?

I stared at his body, helplessly, as he twitched once more
and was still.

With fumbling fingers and the first real unsettledness
that I had felt since walking up to the house, I sunk another
bolt into the crossbow and loaded it. Vampires were everywhere, and I tried to push away the thought of what I'd just
done.

The floor was already stained with black blood, the
vampire bodies deteriorating quickly, turning to lumps of
dark, tarry slag. But the vampires didn't slip or lose even a
moment of concentration. They didn't care that their
brethren were being slain right beside them, never to get up
again, humans or vampires.

I couldn't stop. I couldn't let it bother me. I couldn't
think about it. I couldn't–

Laura dropped two vampires right in a row, their snarls
and cries filling the room, echoing off the marble floor.

Lockwood was still behind us, tossing globs of green and
yellow spell light into the crowd. Somehow he managed to
miss Iona and Mill with every throw, causing the other
vampires to stagger, or the humans to keel over backwards,
falling asleep. I wished that Lockwood was able to reach
more of the humans than Mill had. He was killing vampire
or human, he didn't care who.

Where was Varycas? Why hadn't he made an appearance yet? He couldn't be oblivious to our presence by now. I
held up my crossbow, the weight, tiredness, and the thrum

of adrenaline in my veins making it hard to keep it upright. I countered the shakes by looking for quick movements, and loosed another bolt. I managed to sink a bolt into another vampire, right in her heart.

I realized that I had moved out of the protection of the sun. Laura had stepped deeper inside, too, following the availability of shots, using her crossbow with such certainty that I was amazed. Gregory, too, was now behind Iona, squirting any vampire that came anywhere near her, giving her a clear field to engage any vampire that came her way.

Out of the corner of my eye, I saw movement down the long hallway that Mill, Xandra, and I had been led down the night before.

Jacquelyn.

She looked at me for but a moment from out of the shadows, her brow a tight, worried line. Then she turned and disappeared, footfalls muted under the clamor of battle.

I didn't even hesitate. I took off after her.

I heard my name, but wasn't sure exactly who it was that was calling for me. I didn't listen, I didn't care.

Down the long, dark hallway I followed, chasing blind, angry. Jacquelyn tore around the corner ahead, passing the study that led to the porch. I thought about stopping, about throwing up the doors there, waiting for her to come to me in that position of power.

But I didn't, because I knew she wouldn't. So I followed after.

I looked over my shoulder for a split second.

No one was following after me.

Jacquelyn tore up a lavish staircase, lined with plush carpets and with windows flanking the middle landing. I was breathing heavy as I took the stairs two at a time, but she was already well ahead of me.

Part of me wanted to hurt her, to see her bleed black, to deliver the coup de grace for what she'd taken from me, for what she'd made me do, for everything. I lifted my crossbow and fired. The arrow skipped past her shoulder, striking a glancing blow if any at all; I couldn't tell in the dark. She pounded around a corner and was gone, but I stopped to reload, listening to her stop running just ahead.

With steady hands, I racked back the action and placed the next arrow. That done, I advanced to the corner and slowly slipped around, aiming my crossbow carefully as I did so.

Double doors opened into the master bedroom ahead. It was palatial, with a huge canopy bed against the far wall, draped in gauzy white fabric, unmade with the blankets in a messy lump. From just outside the door I could see walk-in closets, mirrored side tables, and a plush, squishy white rug waiting just within. It would have been beautiful and luxurious...if it had a little more light.

A chill ran down my spine as I stepped up to the double doors. There was movement to my left, and I turned to aim my crossbow–

Varycas was there, dressed in a silken bathrobe. He leaned against the wall as casually as if he were sleeping there. He had a nasty smirk, and was arching an eyebrow. "Well, well..."

Movement to my right made me spin involuntarily, putting the crossbow between me and another danger, and inadvertently turning my back on Varycas. Jacquelyn was leaning against the right-side wall, and now I could see she was wearing nothing but a silken nightgown and grinning at me.

I was surrounded.

40

A stinging pain bloomed along the side of my face as Jacquelyn struck me. I didn't know if it was with her fingernails or just the sheer force of the blow, but my cheek was raw and wet as I slid across the tiled floor of the bedroom. While I slid, Jacquelyn kicked my crossbow – which I hadn't realized I'd dropped – underneath the bed. Then she smiled at me.

I gritted my teeth and came to rest against the far wall. So, she wanted to play dirty, huh? I scrambled to my feet as she walked toward me, circling me like a jungle cat, her fangs bared and her eyes locked on mine. I was vaguely aware of Varycas circling around beside me.

Fear made my skin crawl, and I was trying to keep my breathing even and slow. I was certain they could both hear the rapid *ba-dump* of my heart.

"Where's Xandra?" I asked. Because I was in such a position of power.

Jacquelyn threw her head back and laughed. "Like I'm going to tell you. I will say, your efforts at rescuing her are a lot more heroic than what you did for me. You have no idea the kind of terror I had to experience before I was turned. The sheer horror of what I saw, what I felt...but no biggie, I guess. You didn't come for me. I guess we just weren't good enough friends."

"I tried," I told her. "I had no idea where they had taken you. I did everything that I possibly could–"

Her smile turned cold, all the amusement dripping out of her eyes and leaving her merciless. "Not good enough." She lashed out at me again, this time with a kick that took my legs from beneath me. My back hit the ground, and pain exploded inside of my head like a firework had been let off inside my skull. I clutched at my head, my eyes watering. I had to get up. I couldn't leave myself unprotected like this–

"I can't believe you let yourself get drawn away from your little friends," Jacquelyn said from above me. "I mean, I kinda knew it would work, showing my face, letting you chase me?" Her grin was so...evil. "But I almost didn't believe you'd be that...stupid." She laughed. It hurt my ears.

"Quite right," Varycas said. "Still, she is cattle. And it's rather convenient."

My heart gave a painful lurch.

"Almost like pizza delivery," Jacquelyn said, right in my ear. "But for vamps."

I didn't have time to react. She drove her fist right into my ribs, knocking the wind out of me. I went sideways, grabbing at my chest, trying desperately to draw a full breath.

"What's the matter, Cassie? Are you starting to see why your pitiful human body is no match for my shiny new one?" Jacquelyn asked.

I cast a wary eye up at her in her barely-there nightie, my brain filling with fog as the lack of oxygen took hold of me, then, rather obviously at Varycas in his bathrobe. "I think your new body lost half its value when you let the old man drive it off the lot."

Apparently that was not a thing Jacquelyn was interested in hearing. Another strike met my side, and boy did it hurt. I wasn't sure if it was a foot or a fist, but it was just beside my spine, and the pain was excruciating. My face screwed up, and I was tempted to roll myself into a ball and just pray that it stopped. I had nothing to protect myself; my stakes were spent, my crossbow under the bed, way out of my reach.

"Our alliance is the reason you get no peace," Jacquelyn said. "Varycas knew that you were going to get in the way sooner or later, and so I told him it would be my pleasure to get you out of the way."

I craned my neck around and looked up at her. It hurt. "Seriously? You did a reverse *Lysistrata* in order to get him fine with attacking me? 'Piece, no peace.' God, you're just the worst, Jacquelyn. And kind of a wh–"

WHACK! Something cracked in my side. Still, they were working together from the beginning. I knew it. She grabbed a fistful of my hair on the top of my head, and wrenched my neck back, forcing me to stare up into her wild looking face. Her eyes were wide and manic, so excited about the pain I was experiencing.

"What if we turned her?" Varycas asked. "She might be useful as a fledgling."

My throat was dry, my limbs trembling. My nerves were burning as they anticipated another strike.

"It could be fun," Jacquelyn said, squeezing my hair even tighter, the top of my scalp burning with sharp, needle-point pain as she held me up. "But I think that would be too good for her."

Varycas moved into my view, leaning over me just as she

did. I saw him shrug his shoulders. "I don't know. It would give you a chance to torture her continually, without having to deal with the human frailties..."

There was a malicious flash in her eyes as she searched my face, the idea clearly a pleasing one. Another strike to my legs made me wince, my eyes screwing up. She released me, and I slumped to the floor.

"Your friend here has really opened my eyes to the possibilities in ruling this little city," Varycas said. "I think it's mostly because she hates you and wants you to suffer, but it's possible she's just brilliant and ambitious."

I wiped the side of my mouth, my chest heaving as I struggled to keep a level head. "Oh, yeah, she's a real social climber, that one. That's why she's with you–"

That earned me another strike. I wasn't surprised.

"What you don't seem to understand, little human, is that Tampa is mine, now. And I am not going to run it as nicely as Draven did."

I was having a hard time putting any weight on my arms. The muscles in my back were seizing up, tied in knots where Varycas or Jacquelyn had kicked me. How had I let myself get laid out like this?

Oh, right. Because I was dumb.

"He was far too worried about keeping humans in the dark about us. He would have his slaves, certainly. But he never embraced the vampire lifestyle as I have. He was content with his parties and his showy penthouse. He didn't see the full potential. I own Miami, and now Tampa. If I have my way, I am going after Orlando next. The Lord there is a joke. I could take him out in one night with only a little effort."

"Great, you should go do that," I said, gingerly touching one of my injuries. Still hurt. "You guys can just leave me here, I'll definitely wait for you, no worries. Just hang...'til you get back..."

Jacquelyn struck me in the ribs. "You should be so lucky. Also...you're lying again, Cassie."

"No, really," I said through my teeth. "I will definitely not use that opportunity to escape–"

Another shot of pain, this time through my hand as she slammed the heel of her foot down onto my knuckles.

"I had forgotten how sarcastic you were all the time," Jacquelyn said. "And how much I hated that."

"That's because you have no sense of humor," I said. "God skipped the install on that one. Too bad He didn't miss putting the giant stick up your–"

Ow. Slap to the face that time. Felt like it loosened a tooth.

There was a commotion out in the hallway. The fighting must have spread to this side of the house.

"Help!" I cried, as loud as I could. "I'm in–"

Jacquelyn didn't let me get anything else out of my mouth, clapping her hand over it like duct tape made of steel. I was only able to breathe out of one nostril, and I was struggling to keep the oxygen flowing to my brain. It was getting harder and harder.

The two of them exchanged a glance. "Keep her or kill her?" Varycas asked. "They're going to keep looking."

"I'm aware of that," Jacquelyn said, her grip on my face tightening, her fingers squeezing against my cheeks, making me worried that she was going to crack the bones in my face. I did my best to draw in another deep breath, the sound whistling as it passed over her fingers into my lungs. "Just... stop!" She moved her hand from my mouth and instead wrapped it around my throat, lifting me high into the air.

My legs kicked, and I was wholeheartedly trying to hit

her. Not that it would do any good. I sputtered, stars flickering in front of my eyes.

There was a sharp knock at the door. Which...I had not realized was closed. I drew my darkening gaze toward it and found...yes, the double doors were closed. For privacy, apparently. I opened my mouth to shout, but only a hoarse, strangled sort of sound escaped.

Varycas was smiling as he came to stand beside Jacquelyn, peering in my face. "Catch or release, my dear? Is she going to be the hill we choose to die on?"

"They're coming anyway," Jacquelyn said, smirking at me as I flailed in her grip, trying to catch a breath. "Seems unlikely we're going to find time to suit up and flee into the day before they break down the door, doesn't it?"

Varycas slid over to the dresser calmly, plucking a gold watch from its top and putting it on his wrist. "Not so outlandish. We dress, we leave...we are a bit faster than at least half her crowd, after all. But if you want to take it all the way to the mattresses, I'm quite willing to."

"Think you already...did that..." I muttered. Jacquelyn must have been confused by his comment, because she cocked her head at him curiously."

"Oh, right, I forget how young you are," Varycas said. "It's a reference to a film called *The Godfather*. 'Going to the mattresses' means going to war. Not..." He chuckled lightly. "Ah. Yes. I see. How very droll."

"I don't get it," Jacquelyn said. "What do mattresses have to do with war?"

"Is it a film about discount mattress sales people?" I asked, managing to gulp a breath around her loosening grip. The confusion had relaxed her somewhat. "Is this a movie about a sign spinner?"

Varycas just stood there, his mouth flapping a little. "Truly, you have both just made me feel...incredibly old."

"Awww," Jacquelyn said, a pitying little look spreading across her mean, tiny dog face. "Come kill her with me. We'll drink some of her blood, then spread it on your face. You'll feel young again."

"Yes," Varycas said, nodding and he snapped his watch clasp. "Yes. I think I'd like that." And he advanced toward me.

"Whoa!" I said, with my newfound breath. "Hang on a sec. You know what the difference is between you and me? Besides, apparently, your belief in the age-defying properties of my blood?"

"Yes," Jacquelyn said. "You're about to die...and we never will." She smirked, but it faded as the pounding on the door grew louder.

Varycas chuckled and didn't seem the least bit disturbed about it. "Also...I'm strong? And you're not. I'm wealthy? And you're definitely not. I've got the world at my feet, and...well, you're sort of hanging there."

"Yes," I said. "But also...you have to hire bodyguards for protection." The hammering ceased. "Whereas I...have friends."

And at that exact moment, the door exploded in, splinters flying in every direction, and it felt a little like time just...stopped.

41

An explosion of noise came with the breaking down of the door, as though the battle from the foyer had made its way here, to the master bedroom. Which, I realized as a splinter clipped my cheek, it sort of had.

Mill came through the door grappling with a vampire, the two of them rolling across the floor and into a wall, where plaster cracked and baseboards shattered. Iona was a step behind, her lithe, fully-covered self stepping lightly to avoid their melee. Jacquelyn dropped me in order to protect herself, jumping behind Varycas, using him as a shield.

Laura and Gregory were a couple steps behind; he'd lost or discarded his Super Soaker and was clutching a stake, his expression pure worry at the chaos around him. She still had her crossbow. She held it high, standing perfectly still and straight, and released a bolt. It flew across the room and buried itself in the vamp fighting with Mill. Perfect aim.

Lockwood was a few steps behind; with a wave of his hand he put up one of his magical barriers across the door, preventing any more of the vampires from entering the room. Two of them hammered against the shimmering wall, black blood covering their faces and clothing, their teeth bared.

I staggered to my knees, massaging my throat. I was amazed that my windpipe hadn't collapsed under Jacquelyn's assault. Still ached like a sore throat from hell, though.

"Cassie," Iona called. "You okay?"

"Might need to gargle some salt water," I said. My voice was hoarse, and it cracked as I tried to use it. "Or maybe rebuild the trachea." I felt like pretty much everything was on fire, but I could stand, and I was still breathing. There were probably some sprains or pulled muscles, and I was going to be covered in wicked bruises in a few days, but I wasn't dead. And that was better than I had expected a few moments before.

"Oh my gosh, you're okay!" Laura cried, throwing her arms around me, narrowly avoiding dinging my knee with the crossbow. "I thought the worst when you ran off by yourself–"

"Here," Gregory said, holding out a silver-tipped stake. One of Lockwood's own, capable of harming faeries and vampires. "I see you lost your crossbow."

"Thanks," I said. "And you ran out of holy spritz. Baptism for little Timmy is going to be a real drag. Still...glad you guys are okay," I said, holding the stake up, ready to take on the vamps.

"Did they hurt you?" Gregory asked, jutting his chin out toward Varycas and Jacquelyn, who were still standing against the back wall of the room. Jacquelyn looked ready to leap into the action, but Varycas seemed perfectly content sitting back. His cronies were pounding on the door barrier, which seemed to be struggling to keep them out. Their pointy-toothed faces seemed to be in an endless line just outside.

"I'm fine," I said.

"I thought you said you were done with lying," Laura said. She lifted her crossbow and directed it at Varycas.

"Wait, Laura, be careful – "

But she totally ignored me as she let a bolt fly across the room...and it buried itself into his arm. "What?" Laura frowned, lowering the crossbow. "What was that?"

"It's called 'missing,'" I said. "It's normal...for some of us."

"Uh, oh," Gregory said.

Varycas turned his eyes on to us, pointed, and yelled, "Get them!"

The barrier at the door burst, the frame and part of the wall crashing in as the flood of vampires in the hallway surged toward us in a cloud of dust. I was glad that Gregory had given me that stake. I was sure that the coming fight was not going to be fun, but I braced myself anyways.

One of the guards slammed into me, knocking me backward. He was tall, with broad shoulders and dark, murderous eyes. He stretched his hands and rolled his shoulders menacingly as I got to my feet. Like he was playing with me. Or flexing for a calendar shoot.

I lunged, and he met me halfway.

My muscles were having a hard time responding without sending twinges up and down my spine. My breathing still hadn't righted itself, and my head was pounding. I couldn't keep up. I didn't have any stamina.

Laura and Gregory were there with me, Gregory ducking beneath his arm, darting behind him. Laura raised her crossbow and sunk a bolt in his chest. It took that, plus Gregory's stake to the back, to take him down.

Yet while we dealt with him...the swarm came ever on.

One vampire woman hung low to the ground, reminding me of a spider the way her body contorted as she moved in our direction. Laura sunk a bolt into her collar-bone, and Gregory drove a stake into her.

I was so glad they were there to help. I was even more injured than I thought. Every hastened movement brought agony.

Jacquelyn was worrying over Varycas in the corner. He had pulled the bolt out and tossed it on the floor, the black blood a sharp contrast to the plush white rug beneath his bare feet. He bared his ugly teeth at us and seethed as the battle wore on around them. But the chaos seemed to be subsiding...

Or did it?

Mill threw a vampire across the room and he smashed into the closed shutters, the bone-on-metal action ringing out like a bell in the confined space. He turned on Varycas and growled, very dog-like.

"Now, now," Iona said, her hands balling into fists as she staked a vamp and tossed him off. "Be a good pup, Mill. Try not to soil the carpets."

"Why would you care?" Mill asked. "It's Varycas's rug."

"Varycas is soon to be gone," Iona said. "And I'm planning to appropriate it once he's gone. It'll look great in my living room."

"You have good taste in furnishings," Varycas said, looking at the black-blooded wound on his arm. "Friends? Less so."

Lockwood was suddenly cast aside as if he were nothing more than a doll, striking the doorframe with a *crack* that made my heart skip a beat. In his place stood Alfred, Varycas's chief servant, and he looked...nonplussed. He ran into the fray with a wild-eyed fury, throwing himself at Mill. Fear coursed through my veins. He was stronger, really strong. A lot stronger than almost any vampire I had ever fought before. No wonder Varycas kept him as close as he did.

Iona threw herself at him but he turned at the last second, whipping out a fist that she narrowly dodged. A second strike by her was met with nothing but a grunt from Alfred.

He was easily beating Iona and Mill back, his fists flying through the air faster than I could follow. Iona took a hit to the side of the helmet, snapping her head back. Mill took one to his chest that sounded like a rib breaker. Both were struggling to keep up with him.

Not good. We had come so far, done so much. We couldn't lose now. Not when we were so close to our goal.

Varycas was nursing his wound, Jacquelyn whispering something into his ear. He had pulled his cell phone out, and was looking through it. Like he was checking his email during the fight. My stomach dropped. What were they doing? What were they planning?

"Umm...Cassie?" Laura was looking at me for guidance. She appeared to be out of arrows, and neither she nor Gregory appeared eager to charge in. I couldn't blame them; this fight had gotten ugly.

I heard Lockwood call my name, and when I looked over at him, I saw something flying through the air at me. It hit the ground at my feet with a clatter, and when I bent to grab it, I found myself lifting a knife.

"Wound him if you can," Lockwood said, staggering to his feet. "So they can finish him."

I understood. In New York, the Butcher had been a formidable opponent, having shoved a blade straight through Iona. It hadn't killed her, but it had been effective at keeping her down and out of the fight.

I threw myself across the distance at Alfred, but it was

like he had eyes on the back of his head. He turned to meet me as I brought the knife slashing through the air at him. He raised his wrist, grinning, apparently not even caring as he used his limb as a shield. It sunk into his forearm, all the way down to the bone–

And kept on going.

...What?

What?

What was this knife that Lockwood had given me?

Black blood spurted from the wound as the arm fell to the floor with a sickening *thunk*. Alfred stared in shock at his missing limb, hacked from him by a teenage girl whose strength he had not feared one iota. "I bet you saw that going kind of differently," I said as his stump spurted a black jet, like we'd just struck oil. My stomach turned as the sour vampire blood smell attacked my nostrils, filling the air, and making me nauseous.

Alfred's mouth moved but no words came out.

It gave Iona an in. She used the heel of her palm to snap his head backward with a blow that would have wrecked a car. I was amazed his neck didn't part with his body; it had spun so fast. I slapped the stake into his chest so hard he jerked once, then looked down at it, as amazed as if he'd lost his other arm.

The sound of gears drew my attention to the windows. While I'd been busy dealing with Alfred, Varycas and Jacquelyn had managed to pull out and don motorcycle gear of their own, covering every inch of their previously-exposed flesh. Now, motorcycle helmets under their arms, they were heading for the now uncovered-windows. Sunlight spilled across the floor of the bedroom. They stopped only high enough for someone to be able to crawl underneath and out. Varycas slid his phone back into his pocket; he must have been controlling the shutters from an app or something.

Jacquelyn gave me a nasty look, but there was a hint of smugness in it, too. "Cassie...I'm going to be the one to deal with you in the end. You're lucky today. But that luck is going to run out."

And with a toss of her dark hair, she slipped on the helmet and ducked out of the window.

"No," I said, trying to hurry over to it.

Varycas slid between me and the window, his brow arching. "This isn't over, Cassandra."

"Is this your idea of 'going to the mattress sales'?" I asked. "Because it looks to me like you're ducking out early with your little body pillow or whatever she is."

Varycas shook his head slowly, eyes closed. "You both make feel...so very old." Then he donned his helmet and launched himself out the window. Rolling along the roof, he came up, and, muffled through the helm, shouting, "We'll meet again."

"Or you could just stay and fight now, Varycas," I called after him. "What's the matter? Upset now that I've got friends?" I knew that I wasn't going to stop him.

He paused at the edge of the red, Italian tiled roof. "One less, now." Then he dropped over the edge.

My stomach sank, and with it came a cold trickle ran down my spine. What did he mean by that?

The room was quiet. Lockwood had defeated the other vampires out in the hall. Alfred was a puddle of goo at our feet. Gregory and Laura were safe.

The battle was over...for now.

But none of that mattered.

Where. Was. Xandra?

42

There was a knot in my chest that just wouldn't go away. Varycas's words hung around me like a swarm of flies, relentless and aggravating.

One less, now.

Something bad had happened. That was why they didn't seem all that angry to leave.

What had they done?

"What a coward," Iona said, folding her arms over her chest. "Just bailing like that. He's no different than Draven."

Shows what she knew. Varycas had aims to take over the whole state, and then to make sure that vampires were the ones in control. There was a distinct difference in scope here.

"Cassie? Are you okay?" Laura said. "You're shaking."

I looked at my arm. It was, indeed, shaking. "We have to find Xandra," I said. My voice matched it.

I couldn't move quickly enough. The whole room was spinning, but I couldn't keep up. Not only that, but I knew I wouldn't rest until I found her. I would be an anxious mess the whole time, my skin crawling like it was covered in ants.

"The foyer is cleared, Cassandra," Lockwood announced. "Other than that...the house awaits."

"Okay...we need to break into teams," I said. "And – and –" I swallowed. My throat was dry. It hurt. I couldn't think straight. "And go."

"There could still be vampires about," Iona said. "It'd be best for us to stick together."

I shook my head. "No, we need to split up. That way we can find her sooner. She could be injured."

"You're really pale." Iona gave me a strange look, and sidled up to me. "It'll be fine. We won."

"Did we?" I said. "I won't agree until we find Xandra."

Mill turned and walked toward the door. "I'll shout if I find her," he said, and he took off down the hall.

Lockwood nodded. "I will do the same. Don't worry. We will find Alexandra." And he was gone.

Iona looked me over, eyes narrowed through the helmet's visor. "I don't like seeing you like this."

"Then find Xandra," I said, limping my way over to the open window. Everything hurt now that the adrenaline was wearing off. All those aches and pains seemed to be getting magnified. I looked out; no sign of Jacquelyn or Varycas running across the lawn. Truly, they'd made good their retreat.

"It'd be pretty dumb to leave you alone," Gregory said. "With how beat up you are and everything. The rest of us all need to stick together. We need to stick with *you*."

"Fine," I said, turning from the bright, half-opened window. Pure appreciation for them seeped through the fear that had taken ahold of me. "Together."

"I say we start in the attic," Gregory said. "Or, like, in the coat closet. That's the last place that someone would look, right?"

"Or maybe the garage?" Laura suggested. "They could have her tied up in the trunk of a car. Didn't you say he had a Lamborghini or something?"

"I mean, there's worse places you could be stashed," Gregory said.

"Yeah," I said. "I just...let me get my crossbow. Jacquelyn kicked it under the bed."

The floor was covered in black splotches of vampire blood, the sharp scent clinging to the air as their bodies disintegrated. I didn't envy whoever had to clean this place up once we were gone. Would Varycas and Jacquelyn come back? It wasn't like Varycas couldn't afford another place like this...and we knew where it was now. As Lord of the territory, surely he'd prefer his home base not be subject to constant siege from me.

I knelt beside the bed, my knee popping like an old person's as I did so. The bed skirt was ruffled and pleated, with a higher thread count than any pair of sheets I had ever slept on. My hand passed beneath it, my fingers moving across the cool hardwood floor. My fingers touched something soft, but cold. Not my crossbow. I moved them over the object as I cringed, wondering what it could possibly have been. It felt...clammy. But smooth.

Then I found cold, still fingers.

And my stomach just...dropped.

With more trepidation than I had ever known in my life, I pulled back my hand to grab onto the skirt of the bed.

"Find it?" Laura asked.

No.

Lifting the skirt, I stuck my head into the shadowy realm beneath the bed. The light shone across the floor, barely illuminating...well, anything. As my eyes adjusted, I tried to make sense of the chaotic lumpiness of what I was seeing. I failed, for the most part.

Then...I succeeded. When I saw a dash of periwinkle purple...hair.

What?

I let my fingers dance across the floor, avoiding what I'd touched before and finding, instead, higher, the arm. As gently as I could, I shook it. I noticed the chipped green nail polish on each of the fingers, the little silver ring on the pointer finger that matched the one I'd had given to me, the one with the dove on it.

The flesh was cold. Was still. Try as I might, I couldn't see the steady rise and fall of a chest breathing that I should have been seeing, even in the dark. That shadowed realm beneath the bed was quiet, no sound of breath, just a terrible silence.

I grabbed the arm, pulling as gently as I could. The leaden, unmoving stillness of the body made my heart burn, my eyes sting. I heard Laura and Gregory saying something behind me, asking me questions, but all I could do was stare down...

...at Xandra's face. Still. Unmoving.

But Xandra's face.

Her hair cascaded down over her shoulders and my arm like a waterfall I might have seen in Faerie. The leaking sunlight caught it just so, making it shimmer as if she had colored it with crushed gemstones. I brushed a strand of it from her face. Her skin...it was so pale. Too pale, even for her. The white pallor made my hands tremble as I touched her face. It was like she was made of porcelain.

Her eyes were closed, and for the life of me, I couldn't remember the color of them. Were they more of an icy blue, like the sky in the middle of winter? Or were they more like the sea, with flecks of green and gray?

What kind of friend was I, if I couldn't even remember what color her eyes were?

I cradled her in my arms, holding her body tightly against my own. If I let her go, she would disappear, wouldn't she? If I let go of her, I'd be saying I didn't care. That I didn't long for her to open her eyes, for her to say something. For her to *breathe.*

My best friend.

Xandra...

I had failed her.

I was surprised to see something that looked like a diamond glittering on her cheek all of the sudden. It was a moment before I realized it was a tear, one of my own. It was soon joined by more. I heard a slump from beside the door, and Laura burst into tears. Gregory was shouting something in the hallway, but it didn't matter.

The search was over. My worst fears were realized.

I twirled some of her periwinkle hair around my finger, remembering how just the night before we were sitting together in my room talking about boys and hair and clothes before our big night out. She'd been smiling, laughing, teasing. She'd spent almost an hour making sure her hair was just right.

She had been alive. Vibrant.

And now...here she was, lying still in my lap.

You know, she could have been sleeping. With a surge of hope, I moved my fingers to the side of her throat.

I found something sticky where smooth, flawless skin should have been.

When I lifted my hands away, I found them covered in nearly-dried, sand-like blood. I rolled her toward me and saw that there was a small trickle down her neck, almost completely crusted. I held her against me. I could smell the sweetness of her shampoo, lavender and chamomile. My vision was blurry, it didn't matter how many tears I blinked away.

All I could see was purple.

"Cassie."

I blinked, unable to speak.

"There are sirens, Cassie. The police are on their way. We have to get out of here."

Who cares?

Someone put their hand on my shoulder. Tugged at me.

"I can't just leave her..." I said. Her hair was so soft. I had always been so jealous of how effortlessly she seemed to take care of it. I could see some of her natural hair color peeking in at her roots. She had black hair? How had I never known this?

"You can't explain a body away. You do not want to get caught in this."

A body? A...body?

It was like I was stabbed through the heart.

It – it wasn't a *body*. It was *Xandra*. How dare he–

I turned my face up and saw Mill standing there, a blank expression on his.

My bottom lip trembled, more tears flooded out onto my face, my lips pursing together. I couldn't breathe through my nose it was so stuffed up.

"We have to go," he said.

I shook my head.

He easily slipped his arms underneath mine and started to drag me across the room.

"No! NO, I will not leave her," I said, writhing in his grip.

Lockwood was suddenly there. There were tears in his eyes as well.

My eyes widened. "No, please, Lockwood. Don't – don't–"

Lockwood easily scooped Xandra out of my arms and turned away with her, a single tear falling from his face.

"I can't leave her again..." I said, my head buzzing as I was dragged away. "I already left her once – I can't do it again – I can't – I can't–"

But Mil was dragging me again, try as I might struggle against him.

Lockwood was laying her down on the bed, folding her arms over her chest in perfect repose. Her beautiful hair sprawled across the white pillows, her eyes closed. She looked so peaceful.

She really could have been sleeping.

"No...no, please..." I said.

I couldn't see. There were too many tears. Mill had me halfway out the door. I was reaching out toward her. Toward my best friend.

But it was too late, of course.

Xandra was already gone.

And a few moments later...so was I.

43

It was hard to remember what happened in the grieving days that followed Xandra's death. A lot of people talked around me. There were a lot of tears. Plans were made, dresses purchased. I had to answer some questions, but I don't really remember what I said, let alone if it was coherent.

After a while, I didn't cry anymore, though. I never knew that someone could be so broken by something that they just went past the point of hurting and just...existed.

The world continued around me, but I wasn't going with it, wasn't moving along with it. I just watched it go by, unaware and uncaring of the unfolding events.

Lockwood pretty much moved in at our house after we left Varycas's. Mom and Dad didn't seem to mind. Maybe the added protection of a faerie around the house was as comforting to them as it was to me. Not that I really cared about getting attacked by Jacquelyn or Varycas. The damage had been done.

It turned out that Jacquelyn really did know me. She hit me right where it hurt most.

I stood near Xandra's parents at the visitation three days after we found her. Mom had bought me a nice black dress with short sleeves. All I could think the whole time was how much Xandra would have liked it. I never once looked at her in the casket, or walked up to pay my last respects. I couldn't do it. Her cold and sallow skin was already forever in my memory.

The funeral passed with a blur. Someone got up and said some nice things. Dad had half expected that I would get asked to speak, but I wouldn't have agreed. What could I have said that would have meant anything to anyone? It would have been hollow words, bereft of any weight.

"Here," Dad said, offering his arm to me as we rose from the pews to make our way out of the church. "Just one more thing to get through."

I gave him a fake, small smile and gratefully put my arm in his.

Lockwood fell into step behind us, Laura beside him. Gregory and Derrick pulled up the rear.

It was a hazy day, sticky and hot. The sun was out, as if it were taunting us. Other people were going about their ordinary lives, probably going to the beach or mowing their lawns or going out for ice cream. Our little corner of the universe was not so fortunate.

The hearse was pulled up right out front, black and shining in the setting sun. There was another black car right behind it; Xandra's dad's. I watched as one of the funeral attendants placed small, magnetic flags on everyone's vehicle that was going with us to the cemetery, indicating they were traveling with the hearse and the family of the deceased.

Someone nearby laughed, and I turned to see one of the

funeral attendants walking along the sidewalk, a wide grin on her face.

I frowned. Did she have no decency? Laughing at a funeral like that...

"So sorry for your loss..."

I turned and saw Xandra's mom and dad stepping out from the doors of the church toward their car. She stopped when she saw me. Her dark hair was tied in a tight bun behind her head, perfect and sleek. Her cheeks were blotchy red, her brows were furrowed, and her nostrils flared as she glared daggers at me. I didn't shy away.

We stood there for a moment, staring at one another, the heat of the day pulsing in on us from all sides, making sweat drip down my back, and bead up near my hairline. "This is your fault," her mother said, her face set in a firm expression, but her eyes filled with tears. "You got her into something that got her killed."

Xandra's dad laid a hand on his wife's shoulder. He was silent, but his eyes were puffy, tinged with red. He looked like he had lost all of his will to fight.

How could I respond to that? She was right, after all. It was entirely my fault. All of this was.

Everything these days was always my fault. There was no denying it. No point.

Her mother swelled up like a balloon about to burst, and then just as quickly deflated, dissolving into tears as her husband moved her away toward their car.

Dad's hand closed over my own, which was nestled in the crook of his arm. "Come on."

The cemetery wasn't far from the church, or from my house. Endless green broken by gray stones, each marking a dead person. My heart was hammering as I stared out the window at all the people filing out to stand at the graveside.

This wasn't real. It was like I was watching it all through someone else's eyes. I wasn't really there.

It couldn't be real.

Dad walked me to the graveside where we watched the pallbearers walk the casket to the grave. Laura held onto my hand as the minister read something from the old, worn Bible in his hands. Something about life and death, and how death won't be the end.

I swallowed, the lump in my throat present as always lately.

Slowly, people laid white roses on the top of the coffin before departing. Some were dabbing their eyes at the tragic end of such a young life. Others were stony faced and unseeing.

Derrick eased closer to me. "I should have gone," he said. "I should have gone to help rescue you Xandra. I'm sorry that I didn't have the courage. I wish...I wish I had some ability to help you."

My eyes stung as I stared at his back, his muscles tense. "There was nothing for it," I said. "She was dead by the time we got there."

Derrick glanced at me over his shoulder, and shrugged. "I still wish there was something I could have done." He gave me a sad sort of smile before turning and heading away from the grave, his hands in his pocket.

"I'm really worried about him," I heard Laura murmur nearby.

"He'll be all right," Lockwood said. The wind rushed through the trees, a strong gust sending the branches of the nearby trees dancing.

Xandra loved the breeze from the Gulf. Said she never wanted to live anywhere else.

It tugged at my hair, but the stake that I had slid home in

it held it in place. One of the silver-tipped ones that Lockwood had made for us all.

I would never go without one again. Not if I lived a hundred years.

The graveyard keepers were there soon after, just as the sun was setting toward the horizon, and they lowered Xandra's casket down into the grave. They picked up thick steel shovels and started tossing dirt down on top of the roses and the casket, each crash of the dirt striking the wooden surface like a blow to the heart.

"Hey, is that Jed?" Gregory asked.

I looked up and followed his pointing finger to a boy in a white button down with the sleeves rolled up to the elbows, his hands in the pockets of his black pants.

It was Jed. I didn't recognize him immediately without his hat.

I pulled away from under Dad's arm to go and speak with him.

"Hey," I said as I drew closer. "Where did you come from?"

Now that I was closer to him, I realized that he didn't look so much like a puppy anymore. He was more muscular, the sleeves of his shirt clinging to his shoulders and arms. He had let his hair grow a bit, and it was less like a bowl cut now, just a shaggy sort of reddish. He looked at me with those big, blue eyes and gave me a sad smile.

"I was standing just over there," he said, pointing back over his shoulder with his thumb. "Didn't really think I should be here with the family and everything. You know, since I didn't really know her all that well."

My heart clenched.

"I got a message from the store about what happened,"

he said. His voice was deeper than last time, too. "From one of your vamp friends."

I nodded my head. "Well, thanks for coming."

"Of course," he said.

"How did you even get out here?"

"Taxi," he said. "I'm heading back now. But...I just wanted you to know. If you need anything, anything at all, you call me, okay?"

I wondered how things would have been different if I had been able to get ahold of him before Xandra died. Would that have changed things? Could we have gotten there sooner, prevented this whole thing with just his help?

Probably not.

I smiled at him, but he knew as well as I did that it was forced. I wondered if I would ever be able to smile for real again.

I watched him walk away through the headstones. He glanced over his shoulder once or twice at me, and I was surprised at how touched I was that he traveled all the way up here. It would have meant a lot to Xandra, too.

Everyone left, one by one. My friends. Xandra's parents, after her mother gave me one last, hard look. The backhoe was driving along the road between the graves, making its way toward us. That was the cue to leave.

That, and it was going to be dark soon.

"We should go," Dad said gently, squeezing his arm around my shoulders.

"I need to stay," I said.

Mom opened her mouth to protest, but quickly decided against it. "Do you want us to stay with you?"

"No, you go on without me," I said. "I just...need some time alone with her."

Mom and Dad exchanged uneasy looks. "It's going to be

dark, and they are going to fill in the hole," Mom said. "Are you sure you want to stay?"

I nodded.

"All right," she said. Mom hugged me and Dad kissed me on the cheek before leaving the graveside, hand in hand. I didn't say anything. I couldn't take my eyes away from the grave, filling with shadows as the light disappeared from the sky.

Lockwood stepped up beside me once they were gone. "I will be waiting for you," he said. "Take as long as you'd like."

"Thanks, Lockwood," I said.

He headed toward the gates out of the graveyard.

And I was left there, alone, with the open grave that was cradling my best friend.

44

The sun had set, all of the lights in the cemetery flickering to life. Darkness fell over the ground, painting everything in varying shades of black and gray, leeching the color out of the grass, the flowers at the nearby gravestones, the sky overhead.

I heard footsteps behind me, but didn't flinch. Lockwood was nearby. He would have detected any enemies that could have snuck up on me.

And I was too laden with pain to be frightened. If they wanted to try and attack me now, then let them. I wouldn't hold back. Not when the result of not doing everything I could had resulted in Xandra's death.

A slender female figure appeared between some of the graves, covered from head to toe in motorcycle gear. She wore a helmet, completely black, blocking the light of the recent sun.

My heart skipped a beat, but logic quickly set in. She was too tall to be Jacquelyn. Sure enough, she pulled the helmet off, and I found myself looking at Iona. Her silvery hair was caught in the breeze that rushed through the ceme-tery, flying out in silvery strands behind her.

We stood there in silence for a few minutes. I didn't have the energy for small talk, and Iona was never really a fan of it anyway. "How are you holding up?" she said eventually. Her voice was quiet, reserved. There was no trace of sarcasm or scorn. Just concern.

"As well as I can be, I guess."

"I'm sorry I couldn't be there with you," she said. "I was watching from behind one of the trees."

I wasn't surprised.

"I saw Jed came by," she said.

"Yeah," I said. "Were you the one to tell him?"

She nodded. "I thought it best they were aware of what the latest vampire Lord was up to, the lengths he was going to."

My throat was tight. I tried to swallow, and failed.

Another moment of silence passed.

"Look, Cassie..." Iona said. "I know what it's like to lose someone really close to you like this."

I didn't say anything. A lot of people had been sharing their stories of loss with me, thinking it would make me feel better.

They didn't.

"I keep thinking about how there was so much she didn't get to do," I said. "Like go to college, or get married. Maybe even have a family one day. It was just...too soon."

"Death is a part of life, Cassie, as much as it sucks and as painful as it is for those of us that they leave behind. Sooner or later, death comes for each one of us."

That was a bleak view, wasn't it? "Then what's the point?" I asked. "What's the point in living if all it leads to is death at the end of every possible path?"

Iona sighed and shrugged her shoulders. "That is one of the greatest questions that man has ever asked, isn't it? What meaning is there in life? I don't know, you tell me. Do you still think that you have something to live for? Something that has meaning to you?"

I thought about Mom and Dad, Laura, Gregory, Derrick, Jed. I thought about Iona and Lockwood, and even...Mill. "Yes. There's a lot that has meaning."

She nodded. "Then there you go. There are a lot of things we don't know, but I don't believe that life is lived for no reason, only to come to an empty end. There has to be something more."

"Awfully existential for a vampire," I said.

"I've had a lot of time to mull these things over," she said.

The knot in my chest tightened.

Another gust of wind rushed between the graves, bringing the scent of the salty bay water along with it. The moon was climbing higher in the sky, bathing the ground in pale, milky light.

"Look, I know that there isn't much I can say that could help you feel any better," she went on. "I just wanted you to know that I'm here for you."

"I appreciate it."

"All right," she said. "I'll leave you to your grief. And if you want..." She hesitated. "...I'll braid your hair for you later."

I sighed. "Yeah. I'd like that."

She tossed her silvery hair over her shoulder as she turned and started toward the gate.

And just when I thought I was finally going to be alone, Mill appeared, dressed in a black suit, staring at me, his eyes glinting in the darkness.

45

It was both a comfort and a terrible pain to see him. Part of me wanted to run to him, throw myself into his arms, and allow him to hold me as I cried. But the other part of me wanted to scream at him, tell him to get away from me. The damage done from that night, from his feeding on that man in the alley and leaving Xandra behind stayed with me, haunted me.

There was hardly a sound as he stepped through the grass to the graveside, his vampire, predatory grace silencing his footsteps on the ground.

"I'm sorry I couldn't be there for you today," he said.

The conflict battered on inside of me. I was fine without him there, yet now that I saw him, I wanted him close. What was wrong with me?

"It's fine," I said. There was an edge to my words. I didn't move any closer to him. I stood rigidly beside him, feeling as if there were a chasm there instead.

I couldn't get over what had happened. The last few days...everything had changed. Everything.

"I never should have left her," I said, staring down at the

mound of dirt that the excavator had left. "I should have stayed with her, fought harder to get her back..."

I looked up at him through bleary eyes.

"I know you blame me," Mill said quietly. "But I don't regret saving you. Because if I hadn't, then this would have likely been your funeral instead."

"Yeah, well...maybe it should have been me," I said.

"How can you say that?" Mill asked. "Xandra would never have wanted that from you. She would have been a mess if something happened to you."

"I know what that feels like," I said.

"I...I don't know what I would have done if something happened to you," Mill said. "I've lost a lot in my life, Cassie. You're the first bright spot that appeared on my horizon in a really, really long time."

My heart seized in my chest, and icy anxiety prickled in my stomach.

"I know that something has happened between us," he said. "I may have made you unhappy with my decisions, with how I've done things—"

"It's not just that," I said. "I saw...you. Something in you that I had never seen before."

Mill didn't say anything, but I felt the air between us grow cold and tense.

A monster.

An image flashed across my mind, at Varycas's house. I could almost feel the weight of the crossbow in my hand, feel the pull as I clamped down on the trigger. My mind's eye followed the bolt across the room, soaring through the open air, only to bury itself in the chest of a man...a human.

I couldn't un-see the terror in his eyes, the pallor of his face as he realized he was drawing his last breath. Over and over again, I watched the bright red blood blossoming out onto his shirt.

I was a monster too, wasn't I?

But at least I cared about it. At least I agonized over the deaths I had caused. Mill...he didn't care. He ripped and tore anyone to shreds who stood in his way, regardless of if they were vampire or human. He was vicious, relentless. And as far as I knew, he never even batted an eye.

"You killed a man," I said.

I heard him sigh heavily.

"You killed a man, and you didn't even care. Just bled him dry, right there in the open."

He looked over at me, and for the first time, I really met his gaze.

There was a lot of hurt there, a lot of sorrow and frustration. But anger bubbled there, too, simmering just below the surface. "You think that I don't care?" he asked. "Of course I care. But I care about you, too."

"You did it to save your own life," I said.

"I did it to save yours," he said. "That man on the street. He was dying. I did what I had to do to save you. You and your friends."

I gestured to the grave right in front of us. "Well, you did a bang up job there."

"Don't try to project your guilt on me."

"I'm not the one who attacked the guards at Varycas's estate," I said. "They were all human too, and you just...ended them like it was nothing."

Mill huffed. "I already told you. I did it to save you. And they were going to kill you. They didn't care that you were a human. They were going to do what Varycas told them. He had his hold on those men. And they put their own lives above those of you and your friends. I killed them so they wouldn't hurt you."

"See, this is the thing," I said. "I don't *want* someone who would kill for me. I want someone who would protect me, who would stand by me and try to find the least violent way out of things. You just go in guns blazing, and I just...I'm not like that."

"I tried to warn you that Varycas was not going to play nice," Mill said. "I wasn't the one who tried to make peace with him. It was a stupid idea in the first place."

He wasn't wrong.

"You're right," I said, and lowered my voice. "It was stupid. It's what got Xandra killed."

Mill folded his arms over his chest. "This was the dumbest appeasement since Chamberlain."

I blinked. "I...don't know who that is."

He turned an incredulous gaze on me. "Your education system sucks. Regardless, you should have been the Churchill in all of this." He gave me a sidelong look. "Please tell me you know who that is, at least?"

"I...maybe? Is it another Godpopper reference? With the mattress thing?"

He groaned. "Tell me you did not just mangle *The Godfather*."

"This is just a perfect illustration of the gulf between us," I said.

"The fact you don't know history or good movies?"

"The *difference* between us," I said, "is, most obviously, you're a vampire, I'm not. You've lived through and learned so much more than I have. All I know is the tiny world that I have been a part of for the last seventeen years. You have super strength and speed while I can't even run a whole mile without collapsing. You're graceful and powerful and I'm weak and average in everything. But it's not just that. Try as we might, we have different interests, different hobbies. For heaven's sake, we even have completely different sleeping schedules. There's no common frame of reference for us."

The weight of what I was saying hung heavy in the air. I could tell that Mill was thinking quickly, his mind absorbing my words like a sponge. The gears were turning as he processed a response.

He didn't get it out in time. "This is just...not going to work out," I said finally.

Mill inhaled, taking a deep, steadying sort of breath.

"Vampires killed your friend," he said slowly, meticulously. "I can understand that you can be mad at us, mad at me. But..."

"I'm not mad at Iona," I said. "I blame the beast. I blame the beast in Jacquelyn, the beast in Varycas. And I...I saw the same thing in you. I know you were fighting for me, but...I don't want to be on the same side as that."

The bristly, uncomfortable silence fell again as my gaze turned to Xandra's grave at my feet.

"So..." Mill said, sliding his hands into his pockets of his suit. "That's your final word on the matter?"

"Yes," I said.

"And there's nothing that I could say to make you change your–"

"Please," I said, cutting him off. "Don't make a scene in front of my best friend's grave."

He nodded his head. "Yeah. Don't worry...I'll take it with a stiff upper lip." He hesitated, looking down at me. "You really don't..." He sighed. "All right." He turned with a wave of his hand. "Bye, Cassie. See you around."

As he walked away, the tears finally rose to the surface

again, my heart that was so fragile and splintered already broke into thousands of pieces once more. I didn't even try to fight it.

I knew it was the right thing, but it hurt. I had made the choice. I had told him to leave. I could change my mind, I could call out to him, run to him, throw my arms around him–

But he disappeared into the shadows, and I lost my chance.

It was better this way, I knew. Now that he was gone, as much as I hurt, I knew it was right.

And finally...finally...I was alone in the dark beside Xandra's grave.

46

I didn't think a person could ever feel this much at once. I was like a bubbling cauldron in the hands of an evil witch, watching as she threw vials of different emotions inside; sorrow, terror, anger, longing, loneliness, shame, guilt, all the while stirring them all around with a ladle of regret. Regret for everything that had happened. Regret for ever meeting these stupid vampires that had turned my life upside down. Regret for ever getting Xandra involved in all of this. She could have lived a long and happy life, if it weren't for me.

And like an idiot, I just broke things off with my boyfriend at probably the saddest moment in my life. He had done some horrific things; looking at him had started to make me feel nauseous and angry all at once. But was all of my anger at the situation just completely misdirected? Was he right that I was projecting my own guilt onto him, allowing it to fuel my anger toward him?

I stood there in the dark, aware that a lot of time had passed since Mill walked away. Maybe it was minutes, maybe over an hour.

My legs were starting to get sore, but I didn't want to leave because of that. I could suffer through some discomfort in order for her to know how sorry I was, how deeply I missed her.

The air was still warm, even with the breeze. My dress clung to my back and to my legs, my feet sweaty inside my sandals. My toes were covered in the grave dirt. The cicadas were out and singing loudly to one another, the sound of a summer night.

"Xandra, I..." I started. "I have thought long and hard about what I would say to you if I had another chance. I know that a lot of people would want to give some sort of flowery speech that didn't really mean anything, but sounded good. I just...didn't feel that was right."

I was still holding the rose that we were supposed to lay on the grave. I couldn't bring myself to do it. The thorns pricked at my fingers, but I allowed the pain. It was good punishment for me being the one standing there and not her.

"I just want you to know how sorry I am," I said. "And let you know that...you were the very best friend I could have ever asked for, and..." My lip trembled. "I am going to miss you."

My finger touched the silver ring that matched Xandra's as I stared down at the black dirt.

The mounds of fresh earth on top of the grave stirred ever so slightly.

I froze, taking in a sharp breath.

It was a trick of the light, surely. The wind had picked up. That was all it was. Just the wind.

But the wind had really died down.

I stared down at the grave again, bathed in the light of the moon, and watched as the dirt shifted again.

I closed my eyes, letting out a breath.

I reached up into my bun, finding the stake. The one that I would never go without again.

I took a deep breath, feeling every single beat of my heart in my chest, thudding along in time with the movement of the earth at my feet as something here – something not me, something not my heart – stirred.

This–

This was what I was afraid of.

Cassie Howell Returns in
HER ENDLESS NIGHT
Liars and Vampires, Book 8
Coming in 2021!

Other Works by Robert J. Crane

The Girl in the Box
(and Out of the Box)
Contemporary Urban Fantasy

World of Sanctuary
Epic Fantasy
(in best reading order)

7. Master (Volume 5)
8. Fated in Darkness (Volume 5.5)
9. Warlord (Volume 6)
10. Heretic (Volume 7)
11. Legend (Volume 8)
12. Ghosts of Sanctuary (Volume 9)
13. Call of the Hero (Volume 10)
14. The Scourge of Despair (Volume 11)* Coming in 2021!

Ashes of Luukessia
A Sanctuary Trilogy
(with Michael Winstone)

1. A Haven in Ash (Ashes of Luukessia #1)
2. A Respite From Storms (Ashes of Luukessia #2)
3. A Home in the Hills (Ashes of Luukessia #3)

Liars and Vampires
YA Urban Fantasy
(with Lauren Harper)

1. No One Will Believe You
2. Someone Should Save Her
3. You Can't Go Home Again
4. Lies in the Dark
5. Her Lying Days Are Done
6. Heir of the Dog
7. Hit You Where You Live
8. Her Endless Night* (Coming in 2021!)
9. Burned Me*

10. Something In That Vein*

Southern Watch
Dark Contemporary Fantasy/Horror

1. Called
2. Depths
3. Corrupted
4. Unearthed
5. Legion
6. Starling
7. Forsaken
8. Hallowed*
9. Enflamed*

The Mira Brand Adventures
YA Modern Fantasy
(Series Complete)

1. The World Beneath
2. The Tide of Ages
3. The City of Lies
4. The King of the Skies
5. The Best of Us
6. We Aimless Few
7. The Gang of Legend
8. The Antecessor Conundrum

*Forthcoming, title subject to change

ACKNOWLEDGMENTS

Thanks to Lewis Moore for editing this book. Proofing was by Lillie of Lillie's Literary Service (https://lilliesls.word-press.com).

Cover by Karri Klawiter (artbykarri.com).

Co-authoring by Kate Hasbrouck.

Sanity NOT by Robert J. Crane's family. But I love them anyway.

Printed in Great Britain
by Amazon